The Garden of Evans

Evans

& Other Short Stories

Terry Cubbins

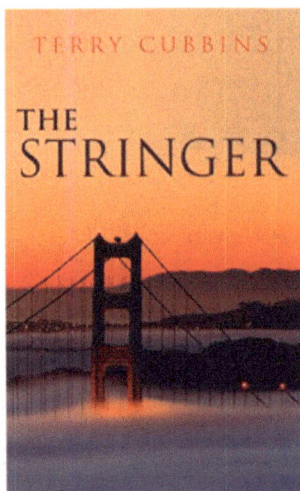

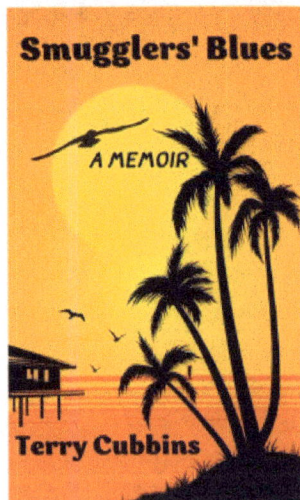

Other works by Terry Cubbins

Find them on Amazon

DEDICATION

In memory of John Molvar.

July 11th 1944 – April 24th 2021

CONTENTS

AKNOWLEDGEMENTS

A special thanks to the following people for reading and helping me to edit my stories. Hopefully you'll enjoy reading this book, but if you don't, I'm blaming it on them.

Al Clasens,
Jimene Smith,
Dan Williams,
Chris Molvar,
Jim Fossett,
Fiona Gardiner,
Bruce Woodstrom,
Anne Wantanabe,
Lynn Hatcher,
Brad Tacher,
Patti Burke,
Jody Hecht
and Stephanie Candish.

7/18/24

Hey John,

Hope you enjoy these
stories

Thanks
FF Cueblos

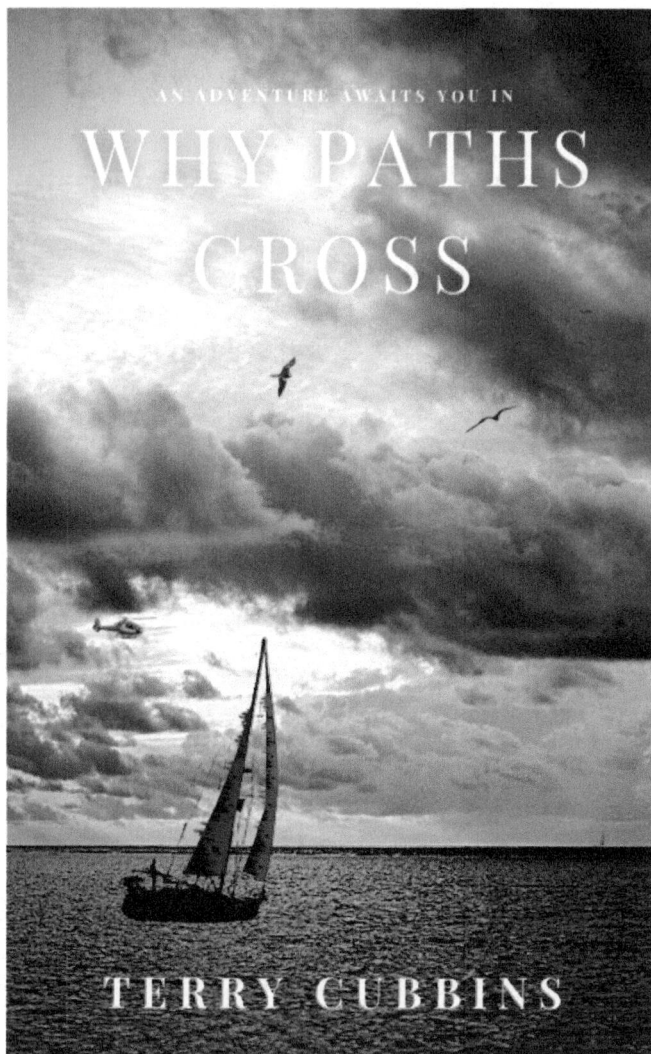

AN ADVENTURE AWAITS YOU IN

WHY PATHS
CROSS

TERRY CUBBINS

WHY PATHS CROSS

The weather off the northwest corner of Washington State can offer a wild ride no matter what time of year. But this day in April, the wind was taking a snooze, letting a cloudy marine layer idle offshore of the tiny fishing village of Seiku. Forty-three-year-old Jeremy Liggett stood on the dock at the Seiku Marina looking at the sign on the sailboat through blurry eyes.

For Sale. 1974 26 ft. Janson. Original main, jib and genoa sails…7hp Yanmar diesel (runs, needs rings.) Head needs pump and seals. 6 yr. old 12-volt battery. No electronics…as is, $1,200 OBO.

Most of the wood on the boat was warped, giving the deck a rippled look and the brightwork was camouflaged by rust and corrosion. The boat, named, Mas o Menos, rode low in the water. Stains streaked the hull. A bilge pump sporadically burbled dirty water overboard. The boat and Jeremy were about the same age but it was hard to tell which one was more weathered. Jeremy had long scraggly reddish hair and a matching beard. The light in his green eyes had gone out years ago. He used to be 6' 1" but then, he used to be a lot of things. Jeremy surveyed the boat and made his decision. The next day he would go to the bank and cash his two disability checks. He'd buy the boat, and then watch the weather. If it held, he should be able to take care of business in the next day or two.

Jeremy Jones Liggett was born and raised in the nearby town of Clallum Bay, population 363. When he was a sophomore in high school his parents were killed in a plane crash and he was raised by his older sister. The loss of his parents was a significant blow to the young man's psyche, but physically, he remained strong. By his senior year he was playing varsity football for the Clallum Bay Bruins and showing an interest in a dark-haired beauty named Laura Tice.

After high school, Jeremy took a job with a local logging company and began to date Laura seriously. After a couple of years of going together they talked marriage and what that would look like. They planned on a cabin/house in the woods not too far from town, two kids would be ideal, a boy and a girl, along with a dog and a cat. The kids would be wholesome, handsome and perfect. The dog would be a Labrador, faithful and obedient and the cat wouldn't pee in the house. Laura and Jeremy would have sex every day until they were old and well into their forties. Their plan worked for a while, especially the sex part. But three years into the marriage and trying to conceive every inch of the way, there was still no pitter-patter of little feet about the cabin. Desperate, Jeremy and Jackie drove to Port Angeles to see a fertility specialist. Laura checked out fine but Jeremy was a different story. His little swimmers were few and far between. Jeremy and Laura were given some options by the doctor, but none of them were what they wanted to hear. It was a quiet ride back to Clallum Bay.

As time went by, the Spotted Owl proliferated in the Great Pacific Northwest as the logging industry slowed nearly to a stop. Pay checks dwindled for a lot of families in the area and times got tough. This wasn't how Laura had viewed the script earlier. This was not how her life was supposed to play out. Then one day, while Jeremy was working in the woods, a steel choker snapped and hit him, breaking his pelvis and other associated bones. At the hospital, Jeremy was introduced to pain meds and when he was released six months later, he was married to them as well. Jeremy had received some compensation from the logging company, but since he didn't really want to blame anybody for his injury, he pretty much had signed off on their first offer. "It'll be enough to get me back on my feet," he said, naively.

Unfortunately, Jeremy's injuries didn't heal as fast as the doctors predicted. Worker's comp became involved but it was evident that that wasn't going to be enough to pay the bills. Laura chastised Jeremy for not holding out for a bigger settlement. His physical wounds were taking forever to heal, while others of a different kind were opening. To Laura's credit, she stuck it out long enough for Jeremy to get around on his own before she moved out. Jeremy, being Jeremy didn't argue with the inevitable divorce that followed. He immediately put the house up for sale and what equity he had in it went toward the settlement.

After selling the house, Jeremy moved into a monthly motel on the only road through town. He tried to find real work, ignoring a nagging suspicion that he probably couldn't lift like he used to and wouldn't be able to carry his load, as it were. In the end, he didn't have to worry about it. Jobs were scare and by all accounts, they were going to stay that way for a while. Most of his friends had moved on, looking for work elsewhere. Even the vampire craze in the near-by town of Forks was slowing and leaking tourist blood.

Three years after his accident, and two years after the divorce, Jeremy moved again, this time to a tiny room behind the Harbor Café in Seiku. As the name suggests, the cafe had a view of the harbor. To augment his disability checks, Jeremy took a job washing dishes and cleaning up the place. The owner of the café knocked off some of the rent as Jeremy would keep an eye on things at night. Jeremy had never been a crazy nor lazy man, but with the opioid fog rolling in everyday, his center of gravity became the back porch of the café. When he wasn't washing dishes or cleaning floors, he sat outside and watched the boats in the harbor come and go, seagulls orbiting and squawking along with them.

Jeremy was in his customary spot on the back porch that day when he saw the man walk down the dock and climb aboard the Mas O Menos. As soon as the man went below deck, a couple of seagulls floated in and landed silently on the forecastle. A few minutes later, the man climbed back up through the hatch with a roll of tape and a small sign in his hand. He taped the sign to the wheel in the cockpit and stepped off the boat. When he noticed the birds, he shooed them away. The birds squawked adios over their shoulders and headed for the open sea. And that's when Jeremy figured out how he was going to kill himself.

The actual thought of suicide wasn't new, it had been on his mind for some time now. But how? A gunshot to the head? God, no. Much too messy. Besides, he didn't own a gun. Hanging? He had heard that there might even be a pleasant sensation connected to it, just before you checked out. But what if he bungled it and left himself more of a vegetable than he already was? Car exhaust in the garage? Out of play there too, since he had neither a car or access to a garage. Pills would work, but then there was still the body to dispose of. Jeremy didn't like the idea of leaving someone else with the unpleasant task of dealing with his dead-ass body. No sir. Jeremy wouldn't do any of those things. He would get a sailboat, a wooden one if he could, possibly the one he had seen the man board earlier. He'd sail it out into the ocean and when he was sure he was far enough away from everybody; he'd build his funeral pyre. He'd stack some bedding and scraps of wood together on the deck below and soak everything with fuel oil.

He'd place a couple of candles on top of the pile and light them. As the candles burned down, Jeremy would be in the cockpit with his music on. He'd swallow his pills and hope he was dead before the fire reached him. That was the plan, a Vikings funeral. No muss, no fuss. He and the boat would burn up. Environmentally friendly. Disappear without a trace. No expensive funeral. Nobody having to think of something to say over a casket. And so it was that Jeremy made the deal for the Mas O Menos.

On April 19, after he finished his shift at the café, Jeremy went straight to his room and cleaned it thoroughly. An hour later, he packed two candles and a CD recorder into a dirty pillow case. He wrote out a note explaining his actions and left it on top of the dresser. He didn't want people to have to go to the trouble and expense to look for him. He took one last look around the tiny room, and then headed for the dock.

At 3:40 pm he stepped aboard the Mas O

Menos and went below to start the engine. At 3:51, satisfied that everything was in order, Jeremy went topside and cast off the lines. He motored out of the harbor with a few birds hanging with him. Fifteen minutes later, when the diesel sputtered and ran out of fuel, he raised the main sail. There was barely a breeze, but it was just enough to make way. For a while, anyway. With the quiet of the ocean, Jeremy sat in the cockpit and steered toward the marine layer of fog in the distance. He let his mind wander. *Will I know exactly the moment I die? Will there be a click or something? Maybe there's a big whoosh just before…?*

Jeremy's plan was to disappear into the fog bank to do the deed but when the breeze gave up completely, he dropped the mainsail and looked around. *This spot is as good as any. Might as well go out in the sunshine. Nobody around.* He sat in the cockpit and unscrewed the top of the plastic container with the oxycodone, tapped the pills out into his palm and counted them. *Sixteen? Wasn't there twenty this morning?*

17

...*Nevermind. He* gulped the pills down with water and then put the pint of Black Velvet to his lips and drained what was left of it. He put his music on and went below to prep the pyre. When he was satisfied that everything was good to go, he lit the candles and climbed back up the ladder to the cockpit. As he stepped out on deck, he staggered a little, rocking the boat... just enough to tip over one of the candles.

Meanwhile, in the fog bank ten miles north of the Mas O Menos, a U.S. Coast Guard MH-60 Jayhawk helicopter, with four crewmembers aboard, was returning to base at Port Angeles. They had just responded to a situation with an oil tanker that had lost power to its main engine. The helicopter, designated USCG 4-3-7, had stayed with the tanker until the ship had regained power and was underway. Now as the helo broke out of the fog, Aviation Survival Tech, Second Class Petty Officer Fiona Olson, was sitting on the starboard side of the aircraft in the Rescue Swimmers seat. She was thinking about the dog she had helped save two days earlier. She thought if they got back to base in time, she could make it to the animal shelter before it closed for the day. She wanted to see how the dog was doing, see if anybody had claimed it yet. As she looked out of the helo's open hatch, something in the water caught her eye. Slightly behind her and to the right, light gray smoke was quickly turning oily black. She put her binoculars on and saw the outline of a small sailboat low in the water. She immediately called the flight deck and reported the boat's position.

"Sir, I have smoke on the water. Five o'clock low."

An instant later, Helo 4-3-7 broke right in a tight turn. As they flew back toward the smoke, the pilot began transmitting on emergency channel 16 trying to establish contact with the boat. Petty Officer Olson automatically readied her gear and checked her harness.

Within twenty-five seconds of Olson's alert, Helo 4-3-7 was five-hundred yards from the Mas O Menos and approaching slowly at an altitude of 100 feet. By this time the crew could see smoke pouring from a forward hatch on the forecastle as well as the one near the cockpit. As the helo drew closer, the propwash from its rotor blades blew the smoke away from the cockpit long enough for Olson to spot a man lying on the deck behind the wheel.

"I've got one soul aft who doesn't appear to be moving," she reported.

The response from the flight deck came, "Roger, that, Olson. Looks like we better put you down there."

"I'm ready, sir."

The command pilot laid out the procedure and the four man crew went into rescue mode. Olson was lowered to the sailboats' deck where she unhooked from the hoist cable, letting the helo standoff while she quickly accessed the situation. She went to Jeremy first and found him unresponsive but with a faint pulse. She placed a cushion under his head and then turned toward the aft hatch. She tried to look down through the opening but was pushed back by smoke and flames. If there were any others aboard, it was too late for them. Back in the cockpit, Olson hurried to get Jeremy in position to attach the sling on him. With the fire getting larger and louder, Olson snapped the harness in place and signaled the copter.

The rest of the rescue operation went per Coast Guard manual and soon both Jeremy and Olson were safely aboard the copter. As Helo 4-3-7 set a heading for Port Angeles, Olson glanced back down at the water. The Mas O Menos was no mas.

*   *   *

Port Angeles Hospital, three days later

Jeremy's body lay perfectly still but his audio receptors were picking up something. A low hum. Not unpleasant, but not fun either. If the sound was a color, it was grey. A few minutes later, his eyes fluttered open, letting in a gauzy, white-ish light. Then a dark shape filled most of the light. Jeremy blinked.

"Well, hello," a female voice said. "How you

feelin?"

"Huh?...feeel...?"

The dark shape came closer, the voice saying, "It's okay, Mr. Liggett. You rest. I'll let the doctor know that you're with us again."

It took a while but Jeremy's senses slowly started to coordinate with each other. He began to understand that he was in a bed. He could see a clear tube taped to his right arm and hand. He reached over and touched it with his left hand. Plastic? Further visual exploration told him he was in a creme-colored room full of odd-looking machines. A black and green screen hummed, displaying a moving line with jagged peaks and valleys. Then, out of nowhere, he felt pain in his head. He closed his eyes again...

It might have been an hour later when he became aware of another voice. It was a male voice this time.

"Mr. Liggett? I'm Doctor Gatkze. Welcome back. You had us worried there for a while, but it looks like you're stabilizing. That's a good sign. I should tell you that you've been treated for some minor burns as well as smoke inhalation. We also had to pump your stomach; you had some nasty stuff in there. But, all in all, we think you'll be just fine. I imagine you have some questions…"

Jeremy swallowed hard and after a second or two was able to croak, "Wha.. happened? Where …am I?"

Dr. Gatkze took a few minutes to explain where he was and how he got there. Jemery drew in a deep breath, looked around the room, and asked, "Why?"

"Why, what, Mr. Liggett?"

"Why'd they save me?"

*   *   *

Four days later, Jeremy was transported to 'Restoration Pride', a non-profit rehabilitation center in Port Angeles, originally funded through the estate of J.B. Musac, a timber magnate who had lost a daughter to alcohol and drugs. The facility was a sprawling one-story affair, nestled in fir trees five miles west of town. The building was well kept and situated on five acres that afforded a view of the Straits of Juan De Fuca. On clear days you could see Canada. The first few days were rough for Jeremy, but since this wasn't his first rodeo in hell, instinctively, he had a chance of surviving, whether he wanted to or not. Ten days in, Jeremy began showing signs of emerging from the confusion. From the staff's point of view, he was progressing physically, but his interest in living wasn't exactly robust yet. That part of him wasn't keeping pace.

Then, on about day 14, things began to change when Jeremy took notice of one of the volunteers. She looked to be about his age, wore her dark brown hair up in a bun, and moved around with a dancer's grace. Jeremy felt an odd sensation. It was familiar, but what was it? Attraction? *Wait a minute. To feel attraction, doesn't one have to feel emotion?* The first time the woman spoke directly to Jeremy, she smiled and asked if he wanted coffee. The twinkle in her brown eyes made something bump inside him. Her name tag read, Nancy Cramer - Volunteer.

As the days progressed, Jeremy got a haircut. Then he shaved. He started speaking in complete sentences, albeit short ones, like, "Thank you," and "Yes, please." And it may have looked like a coincidence, but Nancy Cramer seemed to be volunteering a little more of her time at the facility than usual. Then one day, just before Jeremy was due to graduate, the two of them sat outside on the veranda, sipping coffee and enjoying a warm spring day. Jeremy worked up enough nerve to ask, "Do you have a family? Are you…you know…are you…?"

"Married?" Nancy said, smiling.

Jeremy managed to nod.

"No." Nancy said. "My husband died in a car accident coming home from Neah Bay a few years ago. I was in the car with him."

Jeremy stammered, "Oh, man… I'm really sorry. I didn't…"

Nancy reached over, took his hand, and looked straight into his eyes.

"It's okay. My husband was a good man. You would've liked him. He created a consulting company called Fusion that helped local industries, like timber and fishing, work through some touchy environmental issues. After he died, I took over the business but fortunately he already had a good team in place. I do what I can, but I'm smart enough to not fix what isn't broken."

A few moments passed before Jeremy spoke again. "So, how is it you come to volunteer here?"

Nancy smiled and said, "Because…I was a patient here once myself. After my accident I was dealing with a lot of pain, both physically and mentally. I started taking pain pills, and, well…you know how that song goes. If it hadn't had been for my niece bullying her way to get me admitted here, I probably wouldn't be here today."

Jeremy nodded, took a long time to say something but finally did. "I was wondering, as soon as I'm released from here and find a job, I'd like to, ah, you know, can I buy you dinner… or something?"

Nancy smiled. "That sounds nice, but before we

get to that, I wanted to talk to you about something."
She paused for his reaction, not getting one, she said,
"How'd you like to go to work with a bunch of
people that are making a difference?"

"You mean, like with your outfit, Fusion?"

"Yep. We just happen to have an opening. It'd
mean a lot of time outside, studying forests and rivers,
that sorta stuff. Whadya think?"

"I think if I accept, I'd probably have enough
money to take you dinner."

"Well? There you go."

"Okay, then. It's a deal. In fact, if you want,
bring your niece to dinner too. I'd like to thank her
for saving your life so you could save mine."

"I'll do that," Nancy laughed. "I think you'll like
her. She's in the Coast Guard and she's stationed
here. I'm so proud of her, she's the only female
Rescue Swimmer on the West Coast."

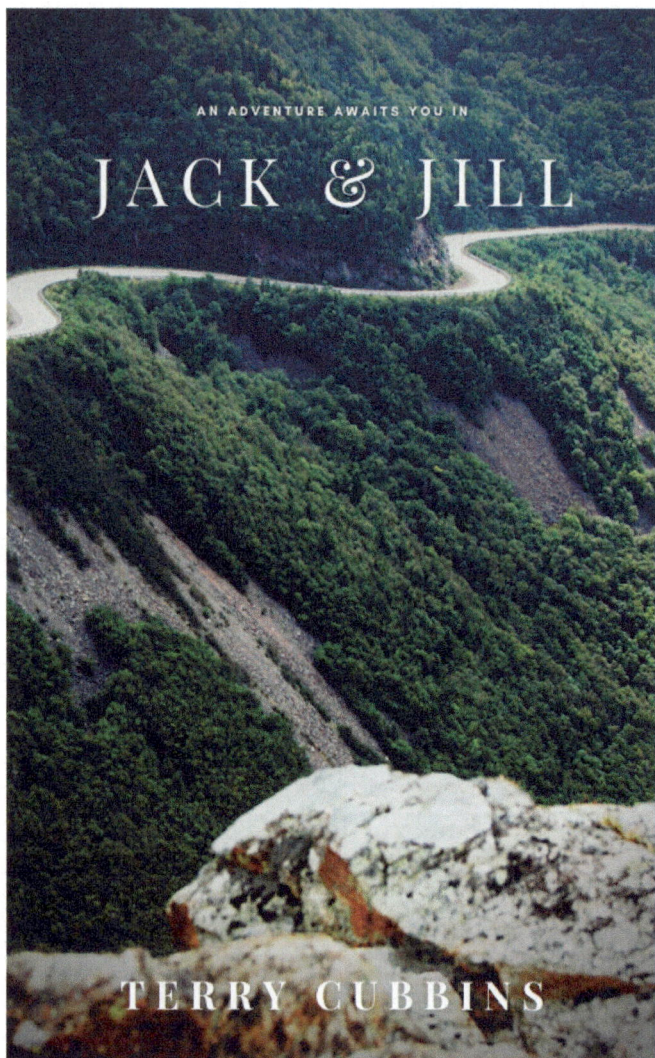

AN ADVENTURE AWAITS YOU IN

JACK & JILL

TERRY CUBBINS

JACK & JILL

"If they do condemn this place, whadda we gonna do?" Jill asked her husband, Jack. It was a fair question, but Jack didn't have an answer. Yep. Jack and Jill. Or Jill and Jack if you prefer. At any rate, Jack and Jill Lambert lived in a funky old log cabin located just off Hiway 1, about fifteen miles south of Monterey, California, or fifteen miles north of Big Sur, California, depending on who's doing the asking. The cabin belonged to Jill's Aunt Sally who had inherited it from a family member back in the 60's. Although Aunt Sally wasn't too crazy about Jack, the couple had been living there for almost twelve years now, sometimes paying rent on it. They shared the place with their three-year old black Labrador-mix, the mix- part showed up as a white spot on the dog's left ear, which made it appear he was missing part of it. They called him, Vango.

The area where the Lamberts lived was beautiful and quiet. They had a stunning view of the

Pacific Ocean, Cypress and Monterey Pines graced the area around the cabin. Their idyllic setting was enhanced by the fact the Lamberts didn't own a television set. Jack had a cell phone that he rarely used and Jill got by with a laptop. The problem was, the land around the cabin was quietly slip-sliding down the slope toward that ocean. The words 'eminent domain' floated through the area. Of course, Jack and Jill had heard just about every going-up-the-hill joke there ever was but they sort of rolled with it, which pretty much fit their personalities.

Jack was forty-three years old, six-foot tall, small beer gut, shaggy beard and long blond hair. He was good-natured, looked like a 60's kinda guy and lived like one. He had an old GMC pickup that he hauled firewood in, selling to neighbors and tourists looking for campfire wood. Depending on his customers, Jack would sometimes include some of his homegrown weed with the wood. He called his strain, Big Surly. But if you asked Jack Lambert what he did for a living he would tell you he was an artist. "And a damn good one at that, too," he would add. He dabbled in watercolors but his main passion was oils. Landscapes, seascapes, old barns, pickup trucks, pastures, and fences, mostly. Some would call him an aspiring artist, which is to say, he hadn't really been recognized as a serious painter yet. He was more of a serious aspirer. His paintings showed flashes of brilliance but he was never satisfied. He'd get close to finishing a project and then he'd just stop and study on it. Mess with it, tweak it, sometimes for weeks. Even when he was more or less pleased with a painting, he was hesitant to sell it. Jack had a flair for painting but he didn't quite understand the concept of marketing.

Jill was still a little hippish herself but that didn't keep her from shaving her legs and looking good. Trim figure, long auburn hair, sparkling dark brown eyes and a great smile. She worked part time at a local gift shop where the owner let her display some of the quilts she made. Jill also picked up some extra money by driving her old Volvo up the road to the country club where she worked as a masseuse. When clients marveled at her touch and asked where she went to school to learn the trade, she would say, "Nowhere, really. I just try not to rub people the wrong way, ha, ha."

Jack was standing by his easel studying his latest creation when Jill came in from the kitchen with two chunks of Big Surly-laced brownies fresh from their little oven. She repeated her question, "So, whadda we gonna do?"

"Well, one thing's for sure," Jack, said. "If they do make us move, we won't be able to afford to live around here anymore… unless Aunt Sally has another piece of land she could sell us."

"Sell us? Dear, we don't even pay her rent half the time on this place."

"I know. Not like we're not trying though," Jack said.

"We could always move in with Aunt Sally at her assisted living place," Jill offered with a twinkle in her eye.

Jack peered over his bifocals at her. "Fuck you."

Jill smiled. "Okay, but eat your brownie first."

Later, as they lay in bed, they continued their discussion. Jill had her head on Jack's chest, twirling his chest hairs in her fingers. "You know, I could probably ask more for my quilts now that winter is coming. I could make a few more of them too. And I bet if I asked Jerry Martin, he could get you a job at the club."

"Yeah, I bet old Jer would like to get me a job, alright. Keep me busy while he makes a run at you. He's been trying to get into your knickers ever since you've been working there."

"Oh, Jerry's harmless. He flirts a little, but I can handle him. And he's always looking for bartenders, you know?"

"Like a steady Job?" Jack looked at her as if she had just climbed down from the moon. "You might as well just kill me right now."

Jill smiled. "It wouldn't have to be like, steady, steady. You know, just come in for a couple of days a week, or somethin'."

"Yeah, right. Like I'm gonna hang with some snobby golfers while they talk politics and tell shitty jokes."

She tugged a couple of his hairs. "Maybe I could sell my body for some extra change?"

Jack laughed. "Yeah, and I'll be your pimp."

Jill pulled a couple more hairs.

They lay quiet for a while, and then Jack said, "Yeah, well, don't worry, hon. I know we're in debt a little and everything, but I'll figure something out."

Jill looked up and kissed him. "I know you will, dear. You always do."

The next morning during breakfast, Jill challenged Jack. "If I start now and bust my butt I bet I could have a quilt done in six weeks."

"Atta girl", Jack said, reading his newspaper. "Could I have a little more coffee before you get started?"

"No."

"No?"

"What about you, Jack? Could you do a painting in six weeks?"

"I don't do paintings, I create paintings."

"Yeah, yeah, I know. But what if we're really gonna have to move soon? We'll need to come up with some extra cash. I was hoping you could turn loose a few more of your creations. I'll match you. Quilt for creation. Whaddya say?"

Jack looked at his coffee cup and seemed to be thinking it over. "If I agree, can I have some more coffee?"

"Yes."

The next few weeks Jack and Jill went about their businesses putting in the hours like they agreed upon. Jill finished up a quilt she had been working on and offered it for sale in the gift shop. Normally for a piece that size she would ask two hundred dollars but this time she decided to put another fifty on it. "Winter prices. Getting colder you know."

Jack was holding up his end of the bargain as well. He would paint for about four hours in the morning before loading up Vango and go on a wood and weed run. After the third week of this intensified hustle, Jack had finished a 20x16 inch oil scene of a solitary golfer on an ocean course as the sun was setting. He called it, 'The Lonely Golfer.' He was quite proud of it and showed signs of wanting to keep it until Jill put her foot down. In the end, 'The Lonely Golfer' hung on a wall in the gift shop by Jill's quilt. Jack decided to play it Jill's way and instead of asking $395, he tagged another thou on it. $1,395. "Like you said, go big or go broke."

As the time went by, Jack took some of his paintings up the coast and placed them wherever store owners and art galleries would let him. 'On Consignment' was about the only deal he could make and then some folks thought his prices were too high.

"You are trying to sell these aren't you?"

Another reason for the added activity by the Lamberts was the impending legalization of recreational cannabis in the state of California. Although Jacks' steady customers assured him they would remain loyal, Jack could read the smoke signals on the horizon. When Washington and Colorado first legalized pot, they set their prices much too high and illegal weed remained the buyer's choice. But once the states' governments figured it out and packaged and priced the product in a more industrialized method, it made it almost impossible for the small farmer to compete.

On the afternoon that Jill sold her quilt ($250) the Lamberts sat at the kitchen table opening their mail. Jill was quietly humming until she noticed the letter from the State Ecology Department. She handed it to Jack to read. Ten seconds later, Jack sighed and tossed it on the table.

"Well?" Jill asked.

"W-e-l-l-, our days are now officially numbered," Jack said. "Sixty to be exact."

Neither one said anything for a while. Jack got up, opened the refrigerator, got himself a beer and then just stood there holding it. Jill stared out the window at the ocean. Vango lay on the floor, his head between his paws, brown eyes peering up.

Finally, Jill said, trying to be upbeat, "Well, we've always talked about Mendocino. It's a little cheaper living there, I think. It's pretty too, kinda like here. Spiritual, inspiring…"

Jack took a long pull off his beer and sat back down. "You know, hon, I've been thinking…"

Jill smiled. "I love it when you talk dirty."

"Ok, here's the deal. You know how artists don't really make it until after they're dead?"

Jill gave him the eye. "Don't tell me you're gonna kill yourself?"

"Well, not really, but if I went off a cliff or something and nobody found my body, they'd declare me dead, right?"

"You're crazy. Shut up."

"No, listen sweetie, this could work. I've given it a lot of thought."

"I'm sure you have, dear."

"Yeah. You get me a job interview with your buddy at the club. I go up there, do the interview and then stay for a couple of drinks, more than a couple actually. I'll act like I'm either celebrating or pissed because I didn't get the job. Then, on the way home, at night, I go off the road and into the ocean. I'll leave skid marks and everything."

"That's wonderful dear. Then I go to the bank and collect on the life insurance policy that we don't have."

"No, you sit around and mope just like I'm really dead. But you've given me an idea, I should take your car, you know, because you've got insurance on it and everything."

"Jack, if you keep talking like this I might just kill you myself."

He smiled at her for a long time. "Actually, I thought of that scenario too, but I think this is better. The really hard part will be to not talk to each other for a couple of months. No phone, no emails, nothin'. You gotta live it like I'm really dead."

Jill started to worry that Jack just might be serious. "You really think your paintings will sell then?"

Jack shrugged. "If they don't, at least we'll be outta debt."

. "Wait, what's my part in this again?" Jill asked. "I hang around here and collect the money that comes pouring in? Then I meet you in St. Louis and we live happily ever after?"

Jack shook his head. "No, St. Louis is too humid. I like the Mendocino idea. While you're grieving...and collecting, I take some Big Surly and go up north and scout around for a place. After two months you start looking in the Mendocino newspaper personal section. I'll post something under the name of, oh, let's say Robertson or somethin'. Yeah, maybe I'll say, "Here's to you Mrs. Robertson, you know, like in the movie."

"You mean, Robinson. Mrs. Robinson."

"Okay. And my first name will be Bob."

"Bob?"

"Yeah. Then it'll be Bob'n Jill went up the hill. We'll be free."

Jill shook her head slowly. "If you kill yourself, I'm not talking to you anymore." She got up and walked out of the room.

Two weeks later they were both at the kitchen table again having coffee. Jack opened the mail and saw another reminder notice to vacate. He tossed the letter on the table, leaned back in his chair and stared at the ceiling. Jill reached over for his hand. "Jerry told me there's an opening for a part time bartender at the club. Said it could work into something, you know, health insurance and everything."

Jack sat forward in his chair back and ran his fingers through his hair. "Would I have to shave and cut my hair if I worked at the club?"

Jill looked deep into Jacks eyes. "Not if you're gonna kill yourself."

The next day while at the club, Jill arranged for the interview. She brought a standard employment application home with her for Jack to fill out. Jack found an old suit coat he hadn't worn in years and took it to the cleaners. He didn't own a tie but found a neighbor who was willing to loan him one and showed him how it worked.

On the morning of the interview, Jack was understandably nervous and even though his appointment wasn't until 4:00 pm he decided against taking anything to calm his nerves. He wanted to be on his toes. Jack arrived at the club at 3:45 and told a serious looking, middle-aged, secretary at the main desk he was there to see Jerry Martin. The secretary looked over her readers and gave Jack a once over, "I'm sorry sir, but you'll need to make an appointment to see Mr. Martin," she said with a touch of an English accent.

Jack refrained from saying, *I have an appointment, you arrogant bitch,* instead, "I have an appointment. Here's my job app."

The secretary took his application. "Oh. Please have a seat, ah… Mr. Martin will be with you shortly."

Jack took a seat and looked around for a something to read. Finding nothing but golf magazines, he squirmed in his chair, fussed with his tie and regretted not having peed before he came in.

Finally, at 4:43, Martin opened his door and looked at Jack. "Are you Jill's husband?"

"Yes sir."

"Fine. Come on in."

Martin was pudgy, about fifty, balding and was wearing a blue tie and white shirt with the sleeves rolled up. His handshake was like grabbing cold mush.

When the interview got underway, they discussed Jack's bartending experience. "I assume you know how to mix all the drinks; Cosmopolitans, Long Island Ice Tea's, Rob Roys, Martinis, you know, the usual fare?" Martin asked.

Jack said he could make a mean rum and coke. That got a laugh from Martin, who said, "Well you got a sense of humor, just like your wife. Man, it must be nice to be married to a babe like her, huh?"

"Huh?"

"Is she a real redhead?"

"What?"

"Ah, never mind. Listen Jack, you do something with your hair and beard and you've got the job."

"Huh?"

"Yep. Come by in the morning and we'll get you a schedule and set you up with a nice red vest and bow

43

tie."

Martin stood up and extended his hand.

Jack left Martin's office, went straight to the men's room, washed his hands and then peed. Before he left the club, Jack looked in at the bar, grabbed a stool, and ordered a Bacardi and Coke.

Later that night, when Jack hadn't shown up at the cabin by seven, Jill began to worry. She busied herself working on a quilt, but gave that up when eight o'clock rolled around and still no sign of Jack. She went over to a neighbor's and used their phone to call the club. She was told that Jack had left the bar around seven, and yes, he'd had a few drinks.

Back at the cabin, Jill's demeanor bounced between worry and anger. He said he wasn't going to do anything stupid, didn't he? He did promise... or did he? At ten o'clock, there was a knock on the door. Jill opened the door and her heart jumped when she saw the sheriff standing there.

"I'm sorry to bother you Mrs. Lambert, but there's

been an accident up the road a- ways. A pickup truck went off the road. Is your husband home by any chance?"

"No. No… Oh, God, no."

Most of Jack's truck was found the next morning scattered down the side of a cliff off of Hiway 1 above the ocean. The County Sheriff's office searched the area and divers were called in. The only thing they found of Jack's, was his cell phone, suit coat and borrowed tie. While others were busy searching the immediate area of the accident, Jill went looking elsewhere; above the Hiway, and around all the nearby parks and trails. When she was sure she was alone, she called out, "Jack! It's me! Your wife! You son-of-a-bitch. Where are you?"

The neighbors could see that Jill was really upset.

"He's not dead!" she told them. "He's just, well, you know, anyway, he's not really dead, okay?"

The neighbors would go away shaking their heads, "Poor Jill."

As the search went on, Jill kept praying that

Jack would appear, apologize, tell the sheriff that he had been thrown from the truck or something. Anything. But as time wore on, Jill caught herself fearing that the sheriff would come calling again. Then, when she thought of everything she was going through, she would get mad all over again.

One day her closest neighbor, Jeanie, came over with some homemade stew and cornbread. Over coffee, Jeanie noticed that Jill had stacked some paintings that Jack had saved. "What are you going do with those?" she asked.

"I don't know. Maybe burn 'em." Jill said.

Weeks later, the official search for Jack Lambert was finally called off. The Country Club graciously offered one of their banquet rooms for a memorial service. With Jill's permission, two of Jack's larger paintings were auctioned off at the ceremony. After the service for Jack, Jill went home to mope and swear. Vango didn't know what the hell was going on. Jill began taking drives around the hills, expanding her search area, hoping Jack would pop out of the woods and flag her down. She imagined him naked alongside the road. Not surprising, her searches were as futile as the Sheriff's had been. Three weeks in, Jill called off her own search too. She was exhausted to the point that her tears welled but lacked the energy to run. She had to find some middle ground between anger and anguish, or face losing her mind.

She decided to put all her energy in believing Jack had really pulled it off. That he was out there, alive and well, waiting for the right time to contact her. She continued to mourn for appearance's sake and she quit telling people that Jack wasn't really dead. And she didn't wait to start looking at the Mendocino Beacon personals. She looked everyday. She pulled up other newspapers in the area as well. And everyday there was nothing.

The only break Jill got in the next two months was that the land around Aunt Sally's cabin had stabilized enough that she received a 30-day stay-ofeviction. As it turned out she needed everyday of it. As the days wore down, Jill was forced to reconsider her neighbor's offer for a place to stay. With two days to go she had all of her belongings and Jack's stuff packed and ready to go. Somewhere. With one day left she opened the Mendocino Beacon's personal section and there it was...

'Roommate wanted. Two-bedroom cabin approximately 6 miles south of town. Great view. Utilities included. Modest rent. See Robert Robertson at 1201 Ukiah Lane from Noon to 4pm. Pet's welcome.'

Jill's heart was racing. She checked the ad again. Robertson? Robert? Then she looked at her watch, 9:37. If she hurried, she should be able to cover the 230 miles or so in plenty of time. She ran over to Jeanie's and asked her to print out one of those gps, mappy things that would take her to 1201 Ukiah Lane.

"I'm looking at a possible rental," was her explanation to Jeanie.

At 3:12 pm, Jill exited Hiway 1 to the west and followed a frontage road for a half a mile before turning north on Ukiah Lane. The road wound through tall fir trees and redwoods. When the road forked, Jill noticed a lone mailbox to the right: 1201. She followed that road for a quarter of a mile to a clearing where a small cabin stood facing the ocean, whiffs of smoke puffing easily from its stone chimney. An older model Jeep was parked in the circular turnaround near the front porch. A bicycle leaned against the side of the house.

Jill parked next to the Jeep, got out, letting Vango jump out behind her. "Okay, buddy, let's go. But stay close now, till I find out what's goin' on, okay?"

Vango wagged his tail and tongue in agreement and trotted off a few steps in front of Jill, glancing back over his shoulder every two strides. Jill climbed the two wooden steps to the porch, paused for a moment, took a deep breath, and then knocked on the door. Thirty seconds passed before she knocked again, harder this time. There was no sound coming from the cabin, and nobody coming to the door. After the third knock, Jill leaned over to her left and peered through a small fixed window. She was startled to see she could look right through the cabin and through another larger picture window in the back wall. She could see a man on the rear porch sitting in a rocking chair. He had his back to the window but Jill could see he was clean-shaven with short dark hair in a military buzz cut style. He was wearing black sunglasses and had ear buds on. His head and chair were moving in silent rhythm.

Jill yelled, "Hey! Mr. Robertson? Hello-o-o?"

When she didn't get a response, she walked off the porch and started around to the back of the house, Vango leading the way. As she neared the corner of the back porch, Vango suddenly stopped, slunked closer to the ground and emitted a low growl. When Jill rounded the corner, she could see the man was still oblivious to her, his head bopping to something in his ear buds. Jill stopped, waved both arms and called out, "Hello? Mr. Robertson?"

The man jerked sideways and looked at Jill. He quickly stood up and took out his ear buds.

Jill took a step back. "Robert?"

When he took off his sunglasses it struck Jill that he looked a little like Tim Robbins, the actor.

He grinned and said, "Please, call me Bob."

Before the words were hardly out of his mouth, Vango barked and charged the man, knocking him down, squirming on top of him. Jill was two seconds behind and jumped on the pile. When Vango went for the man's pant leg, Jill began swatting and punching the man, yelling, "Goddamn you! You son-of- a bitch!"

*   *   *

Later, on the back porch over a brownie and a sunset, the two shared a quieter time.

"So, two of my paintings fetched $31,000 at the memorial, huh?" he asked.

"Yep."

"Then my idea worked, huh?"

"I suppose so."

"What about the other paintings, the ones at the house. Whadya do with them?"

"I was going to burn those."

"But you didn't, did you?"

"No."

"Cool."

"I gave them away instead."

"You what?"

"I gave them away. All except that golfer one."

He looked hard at Jill to see if she was just kidding him. When he realized she wasn't, he asked, "Why? Why'd you do that, hon?"

"Cause I was mad." She returned his look. "Still am, you know?"

After a moment he said, "Well, so, we still got the $31,000, right?"

"Ah, no we don't, dear. I donated that money to the people who had to be relocated where we were near Big Sur. The eminent domain victims fund."

Several minutes went by before he spoke again.

"So, what your sayin' is, we're still pretty much broke then, huh?"

"Yep."

"Did you really save my Lonely Golfer?"

"Yep."

As the brownies kicked in, he sighed and looked around. "Isn't this place beautiful? It's really inspiring here."

Jill gave him the eye, "Yes, it is dear, but I don't think you should be creating anymore paintings. You'll just have to think of another way to make a living and quench your creative juices."

"I've already thought about that."

"I'm sure you have dear."

"I'm gonna be a writer," *Bob* said.

AN ADVENTURE AWAITS YOU IN

APT TO HAPPEN

TERRY CUBBINS

APT TO HAPPEN

Seventeen-year-old high school junior Carl Erskine, was fairly nerdy and like most nerds, fairly harmless. Being a nerd usually meant you were young, male, squeaky voiced, awkward around girls and wore glasses. It was also assumed that if you were a nerd, you were involved in some hi-Tec computer stuff that average folk don't get or care about, like science, math and other giga-thingies. As nerds grow older, they often morph into dorks or geeks who wear black socks with shorts and may even eventually end up wearing bow ties. A lot of nerds tend to be brilliant, but not very big physical and it wasn't uncommon for them to weigh the same as their I.Q.s. Carl fit both the nerd and brilliant profile, weighing in at 151 pounds.

One of the un-brilliant kids at Larkspur High was a bully named Todd McCall. McCall, who was twice the size of Carl and twice as vocal, made it a point to harass Carl at every opportunity. But what McCall didn't know was that Carl was quietly working on a project that would soon give him an edge on just about everyone. Carl was developing a phone app that was allowing him to read other peoples' minds. So far, thanks to his little invention, Carl knew that the school janitor kept a pint of vodka hidden in his broom closet and that his biology teacher was having an affair with the Principal. Carl also knew that Lilly Cranson, a cheerleader at school, had a crush on his older brother, Ron. The invention proved useful as Carl was getting to know a lot about a lot of folks.

It had all started in 5th period science class when Carl's teacher, Paul Blanning assigned the students their science project. Mr. Blanning was a fifty-something, shortish, jolly man with a full head of silver hair, complimented by a matching, full-upper lip. He still carried a slight British accent and the twinkle in his piercing blue eyes helped keep his students awake in class. He was a popular teacher, in part because he explained the basics in an interesting way and offered off-the-wall postulations, some humorous, some bordering on sacrilege, tidbits like, "Would the Earth still spin if humans became extinct? History tells us that when dinosaurs roamed the planet, eating, sleeping, pooping and making little dinosaurs, things were good for them. Then, a big boulder from beyond, slammed into Earth and rendered the atmosphere too toxic for life. Wasn't the dinosaur's fault that they all died. But when they did, the planet kept spinning. In fact, depending on which book you read, it spun merrily for about 65 million years before humans showed up."

For their projects, Blanning suggested to the students that they boldly go where their little pea-brains could take them. He challenged them to 'stretch' their minds in the same manner actors are sometimes asked to stretch their talents. "Let yourself go to someplace you've never been before," he said. "Don't worry, you'll find your way back."

Carl knew exactly what his project would be about. Ever since he was child, he was interested in science and what made things tick, especially in humans. For most folks who study human anatomy, the heart is considered the main motor. Carl was fine with that analogy and as such, assigned the brain as the search engine.

While most of the kids his age grew up playing sports, video games, or exploring their adolescents urges, Carl spent his time studying human brainwaves. The first thing he learned about the human brain was that it transmitted neural oscillations similar to radio waves. That got him to thinking, if radio waves are forms of electromagnetic radiation, why can't a human brainwave hitch a ride on the airwaves outside the skull?

Carl already knew that mental telepathy was not only possible but had already been proven to an extent. In 2014, neuroscientists from the University of Barcelona conducted an experiment by sending an email message to another person's brain in France whose scalp had been fitted with a trans-cranial stimulator. The timing of the signal and the signal itself was kept secret from the intended receiver and contained just one word: *Hola.* When the signal was sent, the person who received the message replied seconds later: *Bonjour.* The results weren't as dramatic as Alexzander Graham Bell's, "Come here, Watson. I need you," but they were promising. For his project, Carl knew he couldn't go around asking people to get their scalps fitted for stimulators, for starters, he didn't know if what he was doing was even legal, or ethical for that matter. Plus, he didn't want to tell anybody what he was doing and subject himself to further ridicule in case his theory proved wrong.

A huge positive in Carl's concept was that he wouldn't have to build any elaborate transmitters or receivers; they were already in everyone's' hands in the form of smart phones.

Carl fussed with frequencies night and day for weeks before finally settling on one that he felt had a chance of receiving human thoughts. Then, flying under the radar, he developed his own personal app for it. Finally, when he felt he'd done everything he could think of, he was ready for a test run.

The day had begun like any other school day. Bell's ringing. Kids hurrying to classes. Some laughter. Noise and chatter. At 8:15, as first period began, Carl surreptitiously set his app to the receive position and pretended to pay attention to his teacher. As the day rolled on, Carl received normal texts and traffic but nothing from his special app setting. Then, at 2:13pm, as he was standing at his locker between classes, his app picked up a pulse. Carl's heart rate twitched. He quickly surveyed the kids in the hallway around him. For a moment he couldn't breathe, didn't want to look at his phone. But he did. And there it was, a message from someone else's' brain:

Jeesh. There's Carl Erskine again. I bet he paid someone to get his locker close to the girls' gym. What a nerd. I wouldn't mind doing his brother though.

It took a moment for Carl to appreciate the situation. Then it hit him. He *was* receiving human thoughts through his phone from someone nearby. Almost in a trance, he watched as three girls brushed past him down the crowded hallway. He looked at the message again. *Yes! I've done it! Oh. Wait. What?*

As he continued to develop his app, Carl learned that in order for him to pick up a person's brain wave with his phone he had to be within a certain distance of that person and their phone. He also learned how to filter out noise and random thoughts so it didn't muddy up the airwaves, somewhat in a SETI manner. But, like most cell phones, there was a drain on the battery, and unfortunately, Carl's app drew an inordinate amount of energy in a very short time. He would have to be selective as to when and where he would engage the app.

There were some earlier tests that Carl thought were successful but somewhat embarrassing. Like the time he was in the supermarket express checkout line. There was one man in front of him when he tapped on his app. He waited two seconds before looking down at his phone:

What's with this kid behind me? He's in my space. Counting how many items I have? God, I hate close- standers.

Another time came when Carl was talking to his English teacher with the app engaged:

Hmm, kinda hard to look at Carl with that booger hanging in his nose.

But the ping that changed everything came one day just before Mr. Banning's science class. Carl was walking down the hall behind Amy Coltrane, the girl who sat across from him in class. Amy was a cutie, no doubt about it. Long dark brown hair. Large brown eyes. Dimples when she smiled. Nice figure. Nice person. A lot of boys pursued Amy and she had gone out with a few of them, but nothing worked into anything steady. Amy seemed more interested in school projects and keeping her grades up than playing with boys her own age. She had the normal urges of a young female but she was determined to lose her virginity on her own terms. Just as Amy reached the classroom door, Todd McCall appeared out of nowhere and grabbed her arm. "Hey, Amy. How ya doin?" It was clear from Amy's expression she was not happy to see him. When she pulled her arm away, McCall said, "Aw, come on now. How come you won't talk to me?"

Carl slowed, tapped on his app and walked toward the entry door. McCall noticed him coming, looked away from Amy, then to Carl; "Where you think you're goin', dickweed?"

Carl put his head down and tried to squeeze around the two. He was just about past them when McCall wacked him on the back of his head, sending his glasses flying to the floor. When Carl reached down for his glasses, McCall kicked him in the butt, knocking Carl down on top of his glasses. McCall laughed, "You should look where you're goin,' stupid."

Amy immediately pushed McCall away and rushed

to Carl's aid. Kneeling next to him, she asked, "Are you okay?" But before Carl could answer, Amy snapped her head back to McCall and snarled at him. "You jerk. Leave him alone. Just get outta here."

As McCall laughed and walked away, Amy helped Carl to his feet and then bent down and gathered up what was left of his glasses. Before she turned to go to her seat, Amy smiled and said, "I hate bullies, don't you?"

After he dusted himself off and settled into his seat, Carl peeked at his phone. He had to squint but he made out the message:

I never noticed Carl's eyes before. They're really blue. Hmm.

When Carl first looked at the text he was delighted to see that he had scored another hit. He made a note to log the data as he had done with all the others stating the clarity, the amount of battery drain and the who, what, why, where and when.

The next morning, Carl studied all of the

random texts he had received up to that point. Besides the ones mentioned earlier, entries included:

Boy, I gotta pee...
Wonder if I have enough gas to get home...
This test shouldn't be too hard...
Look at those tits...

So far, Carl hadn't found anybody thinking of robbing a bank or murdering someone. Mostly just blathering, sub-conscious waves that didn't make much sense, almost like dreams sometimes do. Other thoughts came across as songs and humming.

Carl contemplated his next move. Was it time to show his work to someone? Mr. Blanning? His father? A patent attorney? In the end, he decided he should do some more experimentation before any disclosure. He didn't want his project taken over by someone who might not share his goals or enthusiasm. As far as he was concerned, it was one thing to get to the moon, it was another to explore it. After much thought, Carl decided that in the interest of science and common sense, he should focus on Amy. She was a static target sitting right next to him a lot of the time. He could conserve power and work out some of the bugs on her. The thought occurred to him that what he was doing might seem a little peeping Tom-ish, invading her privacy and all. Literally bugging her. Reading her naked thoughts. So, again, after much thought, and in the interest of science, Carl pushed that thought into a corner for the time being.

Then he considered Todd McCall. Carl was sure he could spare enough airtime on the bully's frequency to find his kryptonite. It was one day in the school's cafeteria that Carl was able to take advantage of an impromptu seating arraignment that had McCall sitting directly across from him at lunch. When a classmate passed a food tray in front of McCall and McCall recoiled away from it, Carl thought he may have just gotten a clue. When he looked at his phone, he knew he had his man. McCall was suffering from Arachibutyrophobia. You read right. McCall had a fear of… peanut butter. From that day forward, Carl's backpack always contained a peanut butter sandwich and lots of his new favorite snack, peanut butter and crackers.

Over the next few weeks' Amy became aware of subtle differences in Carl. Besides not wearing his glasses anymore, it looked like he was letting his hair grow longer. She also noticed he wasn't wearing the same blue short-sleeve shirt with the pocket protector that he used to wear every day, in fact, his entire wardrobe seemed to be slowly evolving, different shirts and pants that seemed to fit him better. Then the real surprise came when he asked if she needed any help with her science project. It was as if he was reading her mind or something.

The first time Amy and Carl studied together, they did so at her house. After introductions were made to her parents, Amy led Carl to her father's study and pulled two overstuffed chairs close together. With their knees almost touching, Amy smiled and asked, "Ready?"

Carl detected a faint, sweet perfume and when he looked into her eyes, he felt something begin to churn in him that he'd never felt before.

Amy asked again, "Carl?"

"Uuh? ah, yeah, sure, okay."

When Carl reached for his phone, Amy put her hand on his arm. "Sorry, no phones allowed in the study. Daddy's rules."

Carl blushed and put his phone away.

"Thanks," Amy said. "Daddy says we spend way too much time staring at the damn things. He says we should be seeing what's going on around us. It's a generational thing, I think."

At first, Carl was upset that he wouldn't be able to connect with Amy's thoughts but as their study session progressed he grew more comfortable. On one occasion when Amy laughed at something silly, Carl's mind slipped for a moment and he imagined being married to her and living in a house like the one they were in.

Three days later, Amy and Carl had just settled into their seats for science class when Mr. Blanning came into the room, walked to the blackboard with a piece of chalk and wrote out the word; 'Inventions,' then he turned around and surveyed his audience. One of Mr. Blanning's traits was to start his lectures off with a proverb that he would work into the topic at some point. The proverb was usually an original that had been handed down by his father, Peter, who had been a farmer in Iowa. The adage would typically refer to farming and equipment but Blanning would massage it to fit his needs in the classroom. When Blanning was sure he had everybody's attention he threw out the clue; "As my father used to say, 'Never start a piece of equipment unless you know how to shut it off first."

Blanning let that float out there for a couple of beats and then he began his homily.

"Today we'll be talking about inventors and their inventions, or discoveries, if you prefer. Inventions like the automobile for example. That's definitely something you should know how to shut off before starting it, right? Well, in 1886 Karl Benz received a patent for a vehicle powered by a gasoline engine, or as most saw it, the first-ever car. It was a three-wheeler with one bench seat and had a top speed of 10 miles per hour. On dirt. Benz probably didn't see the need for a seat belt or even a back seat at the time, sorry, kids."

As some of the students rolled their eyes and snickered, Amy looked over at Carl and smiled. Carl returned the favor and then instinctively tapped his app as Blanning kept his theme going.

"Later, in 1913 when Henry Ford started rolling off Model T's every two and a half hours, he wasn't thinking about air pollution or about people slamming into each other with his cars, Henry was counting the money. The term, 'Climate-change' wouldn't be coined for another eighty years, or so."

Oh, gawd. I hope don't lose my virginity in the back seat of a car. How could you even do it in a Mini-Cooper like Carl's?

"Another inventor who deserves our attention is

none other than, Leo Baekeland. Who, you ask? Well, ole Leo might not be a household name, but in 1907 he invented something that's in every household today. In fact, in the 60's it was the 'in' word. If you've ever seen the movie, *The Graduate*, you know which product I'm talking about. That's right – plastic! And when Leo declared his invention to be nearly indestructible he was virtually spot-on. How would he know at the time that there'd come a time when we would have to think of ways to dispose of his invention? Today, plastic is still the 'in' word, as in everything; in landfills, in oceans and in bellies of fish."

I wonder if Carl carries a condom? He's probably still a virgin. I hope.

"Another interesting discovery that we're still wondering about is nuclear energy. In the mid 1930's, when Enrico Fermi showed the world that it was possible to create energy by splitting atoms, could he have ever imagined Hiroshima? Nagasaki? Or even

Three-mile island? Chernobyl? And how could Fermi have ever guessed that one day plutonium would help power a spacecraft such as Voyager One, into space for a one-way trip through the universe in search of other life? And because metal and machines last longer than human flesh, Voyager One could be traveling for the next 40,000 years, or till the end of time for that matter. It's interesting to think that mankind put heart and soul into a machine that has neither."

Hmm...that's kinda creepy when you think about it.

"Then let's say an alien form of life does connect with Voyager and the plutonium doesn't contaminate everything in sight; what will it think of our little spiny contraption? Besides the plutonium on board, we left other calling cards; a drawing by DaVinci to show the extraterrestrials what us humans look like, and a golden disk record with ditties by Mozart and Chuck Berry to give the aliens an inkling of our musical tastes. And what if these aliens are able to trace the Voyager's path back to Earth? What will they find? A bunch of people with chips in their heads telling them how to move their lips? Robots? Computer families? We already have trains, planes and automobiles that drive themselves. Goodness, for all we know, Alexa and Siri may have already mated and are now happily on their way to making people obsolete."

I think Carl likes country music.

Blanning took a deep breath and then began to wrap things up. "Obviously we can't un-invent the things we've been talking about today," he said. "Nor would we want to, but unless we pay attention and watch what we're doing, we might just evolve ourselves right into extinction. Begging the question: If the human race falls in the forest and there's no one to hear it fall, will it make a noise?"

The silence that followed just accentuated his question. Some students smiled and looked at each other.

"So, what I want you to think about is this; you are the next generation of humans. Please keep hearts and souls involved in what you do. Embrace technology but don't let it get away from you."

Carl looked down at his phone:

I wonder if Carl will give me a ride home after school today. He still hasn't told me what his science project is about.

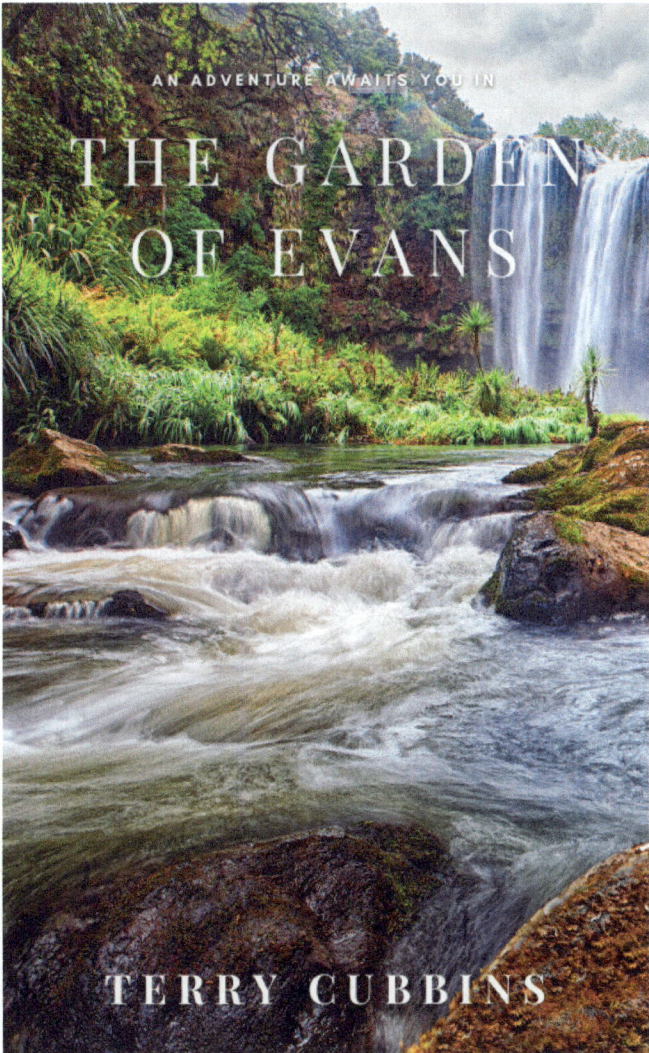

AN ADVENTURE AWAITS YOU IN

THE GARDEN OF EVANS

TERRY CUBBINS

THE GARDEN OF EVANS

Doc Evans could remember when there was a sand beach near his macadamia farm on the Big Island. His wife and two kids used to go there for picnics. The farm was near the tiny town of Lau, which consisted of a general store, school and post office. An annual rainfall of a hundred-twenty inches and an occasional active volcano helped keep the population down. That was before climate change of course. Before the ice caps melted and Earth's natural ingredients of floods, fires, droughts and hurricanes, were accelerated by man. Fortunately, the Evans farm had escaped most of the effects of global warming. Twenty acres of macadamia trees were ringed with heavy foliage, palms and tropical hibiscus. From the back porch of the house, you could follow a stream that ran through the property down to the ocean. From the front steps you could follow it back up the mountain past waterfalls, pools and caves.

Doc and his wife, Carla, didn't need the farm to survive. Carla was a radiologist who worked part time at the hospital in Hilo and Doc, was a noted astrophysicist who had warned of an impending weather transformation years ago. He would say, "Theoretically, if there were enough bridges, a person could walk twenty-five thousand miles around the circumference of Earth. But if he or she tried to walk straight up for five miles, he or she would die from lack of oxygen. Our blanket of life is really thin."

Doc was in charge of the Mauna Kea Observatories on Hawaii and spent most of his work-week peering through a giant telescope. You'd thought that someone who commanded such an instrument would've commanded more of a listening audience when it came to the atmosphere.

Unfortunately, many people thought global warming was a hoax. Unbridled, they kept multiplying while going forth. All in all, the planet was a mess. The tenants, all twelve billion of them, had let the place go. The political climate was also just as wobbly. Thirty-three nations had long-range nuclear missiles. The countries that didn't have nukes were online trying to build one. Mexico still didn't have a wall but they had a silo. Sadly, people couldn't figure things out as the situation neared the tipping point. As motorist Rodney King once asked the L.A. cops after they beat the shit out of him, "Can't we all just get along?" It was a simple question. And he wasn't insinuating you had to like the other guy's music or stay in touch or anything. Just be cool. Just, you know, *get along*. Citizenry missed an opportunity when they didn't elect Rodney, king of the world.

Meanwhile, as all 4,312 religions chanted, "We're number one," Iran flipped off Iraq. Russia called Turkey a pig farm. Palestinians booed Israelis. Somalia pissed everyone off with their campaign, *Used Yachts R Us*. Even Canadians were getting cranky about something.

However, nothing took the joy out of living for the Evans' children. Their daughter, Sara, matured into a lovely young lady and married a local boy named Andy Logan. Andy was a quiet young man who grew up helping his father on his fishing boat.

When plastic in the ocean began to outnumber fish, Andy's dad converted his boat to corral the trash and sell it to the Blue Ocean Society. Unlike fish, there was no limit on plastic and you could fish for it year-round. When Andy took time away from the sea, he lived on the farm and helped work the macadamia. The Evans' son, Casey, worked on the farm as well, but lived in town with Jenny, the funny little redhead that had been his steady since the fourth grade. Casey was good-looking, polite, hard working and always seemed to be smiling. His happiness could be directly attributed to Jenny who was a real cutie-pie herself and could sing like a bird.

But that was all before Doc called a family meeting one night and let them in on a little secret; for months he had been tracking a giant asteroid that had emerged from deep space. The U.S. had been mining asteroids for years but this one, besides being humungous, seemed to be made up of a mysterious material. It appeared to *attract* radiation rather than *dispersing* it. Asteroid # 2329 E (E for Evans) had the profile of a stealth bomber and was behaving like one.

And if Doc's calculations were correct about the asteroid's flight path, people on Earth had about eighteen months to live. Once this little tidbit went public, folks went ballistic, "Are you sure? What about a second opinion? Is this like the climate-change-hoax- thingy? Oh, wait a minute... so, anyway, wadda we gonna do?"

Of course, everybody remembered what Hollywood did. They simply sent Bruce Willis and his cosmos cronies up to the annoying asteroid, placed a nuclear bomb on it, and high-tailed it back to Earth. Ka-fucking-blooey. Problem solved. But that was Hollywood and this was real. Scientists scrambled for a solution: Maybe fly a few chosen ones and their pets to the Moon Port until the dust settles? Build Cold War style bunkers? Resume the search for the Lost City of Atlantis? Prayer? "Excuse me, God? I know you're busy, but is this really what you want here? Is this your *will?*

Emergency meetings of NATO were called to explore further options. After weeks of hurried squawking, leaders voted to go with the, 'bomb-the-shit-out of it' option,' the way Bruce and his boys did it. However, Houston, there *was* a problem. As asteroids go, # 2329 E was bigger than anything astronomers had ever seen. If this bad boy was going to be redirected, a really powerful bomb, or more likely, *bombs*, would be needed. But which country should get the contract for saving the World? Who had the biggest bomb? Who had the most nukes? Which nation had the most experience in this sort of thing? The usual suspects were Russia and the U.S. but China had to be considered as well. China argued early in the 1980's that if the human population continued to grow unchecked, the lifeboat wouldn't big enough for everyone. Hence, China spent a lot of time on rocket propulsion and guidance. A coalition was formed to put a game plan in motion. The first thing asked, "If something needs the shit blown out of it, who you gonna call?"

They all agreed that America was the go-to country in that category. But there was another thing that had to be established; if America was going to give up its best stuff to save the world, the world would have to agree to not take advantage of the situation. NATO quickly wrote up a treaty declaring that no country could make war against the United States for at least ten years after the asteroid was successfully dealt with. There were no provisions for a failed mission.

Meanwhile, Doc was making his own contingency plans for his family. He favored the 'hunker-in-a-bunker' method. Optimistic entrepreneurs offered specials on custom-made fortification units, but they were very expensive. That's when Sara wondered if maybe one of the caves along the stream east of their farm might work just as well. Doc immediately thought of the cave where the kids used to go pretending they were hiding from pirates. It was directly behind a waterfall and had an opening diameter of about three feet. However, once inside, the cave opened up enough to stand up in and went back another thirty-feet. A family plan was laid out. They would remodel what the cave would allow. Throw in some mattresses and store enough provisions to last a month or so. Among those provisions were two semi-automatic rifles and two thirty-eight-caliber handguns with ammunition.

As time passed Doc continued to monitor 2329 E. With six months to go, rockets were readied and payloads collected. At the three-month mark, the countdown began in earnest. While all of this was going on much of the world tried to put on a brave face, after all, there had been doomsday predictions before.

In the year 1216, Pope Innocent claimed the world would end 666 days after the rise of Islam. Christopher Columbus had his money on 1658. The Jehovah Witnesses bet on a day in 1941, but when that date came and went, the Jay Dubs re-figured and hung their hopes on something in 1975. They're working on another one as we speak. The only person to seemingly nail it was Jim Jones, The People's Temple leader, when he predicted November 18, 1978, as D Day. Yet, history gives him an asterisk: to ensure his prediction, the Right Reverend mixed up some un-cool-aid and took 971 culties with him in that day in Guyana. And then Nostradamus's earlier pick of 1999 missed the mark. The Y2K thing. The Mayan Calendar...yada, yada, yada. Besides whadda you gonna do? Bets were made.

"We're not gonna die," said one golfer.

"Oh, yeah?" challenged his partner. "Five bucks says we do."

Las Vegas offered 500-1 against. They didn't get many takers, but there were a few. Then, with about a month to go, Doc discovered that 2329 E had somehow picked up speed and was closing faster than originally thought possible. Because of 2329 E's revised ETA, China, who was in charge of photographing the whole shebang, furiously scrambled to launch their recon satellite ASAP.

However, it wasn't until after the Chinese lit the candle on their rocket that they remembered they had forgotten to tell anyone what they were doing and *when*. North Korea's' early warning system computers detected China's rocket launch and clicked into defense mode, albeit with the safety on. North Korea's Computer- in-Charge immediately asked it's other computers, "Say, Hal. You think what we're seeing here fits the criterion for a, you know, retaliation? And if so, when and where?"

This was all happening at a time when many people believed that computers had evolved to the point that they had souls. They could be influenced slightly by human traits, even assimilating music and paranoia. Hundred-year-old songs like, "For What It's Worth," by The Buffalo Springfield, may have seeped through the motherboard.

There's something happening here,
What it is, ain't exactly clear.
There's a man, with a gun over there,
Telling me, I got to beware.

Unfortunately, before a human could intervene, Hal flipped the safety and fired a salvo at China. A computer heartbeat later, China's machinery responded in kind. Russia's system sensed something and pulled the trigger, sending it's best to America. U.S.'s fail-safe program detected an incoming and fired at Venezuela. England bombed North Africa.

Egypt squeezed off a few at Israel. Mexico lobbed their nuke and hit Texas.

Paranoia strikes deep. Into your life it will creep

As all this began, Carla had her lab coat on and was about to leave for a work. She and the rest of the family had just finished rehearsing their asteroid survival plan at the farm when the kitchen radio began bleating an automated emergency warning signal, "We interrupt this broadcast with important news. Reports out of Washington indicate that North Korea has launched a missile attack on China. China allegedly has responded. Additional sources say satellites have picked up other action around the globe ..." The radio crackled and popped. "Stay tuned as we ar..." Then *bloop*, nothing.

Nine minutes later, Andy, Jenny, and the rest of the Evans family squeezed into the cave. When they switched on their lantern, they were surprised to find they were not alone. In a far corner, teenagers Laura Jones and Eddie Wain were literally caught with their pants down. They quickly jumped up and zipped up.

"Oh, hi. We were just, you know, ah, leaving…" said Eddie. Apparently, Eddie had told Laura it was okay to do the big naughty since they were going to die soon anyway. "Wait a minute," Eddie said, "Whaddya guys doing here? Did the asteroid come?"

"No," Doc answered, "but nuclear war may have just started. Everywhere." As if on cue a siren started wailing followed by loud booming sounds.

"Oh my god!" Eddie looked at Laura. "We better get home."

"Wait," Carla said, as she pulled the radiation badge off of the lapel on her lab coat. "We've already been exposed." Nobody said a word for several seconds. Then Carla reached in her pocket. "I have extra vials for the badge. I'll swap this one out and see what it reads in here, where we are now."

Everyone watched as Carla changed out the dosimeter and to their relief, the reading was much lower. Casey looked over Carla's shoulder to read the dosimeter herself. "Is it lower because we're in a cave?"

"Maybe. The lava rock might be absorbing some of the radiation, I don't know," Carla shrugged.

Doc walked over to the entrance of the cave to take a look at the outside. "I think we better stay inside for at least twenty-four hours." He rolled a rock over to the entrance. "There. That's our front door for now."

The next morning, dirty orange light filtered in around the rock. The air smelled like burnt rubber. Nobody had slept. They were tired and scared, but alive. To test the radiation level outside the cave, Carla used fishing line from their survival kit, tied it to her badge and tossed it outside. When she reeled it in, the dosimeter was still hot. With a new vial she checked the level inside the cave; it had moved up only slightly.

One week later, readings outside the cave were the same, and inside, the radiation level was beginning to creep up. Morale sucked. Then, asteroid 2329 E came calling. Everyone's ears started popping, followed by a sensation like their brains were being sucked out through their ears. They scrambled out of the cave like it was a burning building. A dark mass which seemed the size of Montana was quickly moving directly over them. In front of the shape the sky was still dirty orange, but behind it was a wake of blue skies. In seconds the monster disappeared over the western horizon followed by a huge sonic BOOM that shook the ground.

The sucking sensation was suddenly gone. The air, fresh and clean... Carla looked at her husband, "My God! What was that?"

"I'm not sure dear, but my guess is that was twenty-three- twenty-one, the asteroid that was supposed to hit us. I must have miscalculated something," and he almost sounded apologetic. "However, I think it may have just hoovered the air for us." To test his theory, Doc drew in a deep breath, picked up a banana, peeled it and ate it. He drank from the stream and peed freely.

At first the cave dwellers were ecstatic, but as they began exploring their environs, they realized that crying time had only just begun. Most of their farmhouse was gone and when they started toward Lau they saw skeletons littering the landscape. Laura, Eddie, Jenny and Andy, searched the area where their parents lived but found nothing but bones amid wreckage. They trekked to Hilo, but found more of the same. Most of the boats in the harbor had either sunk or been tossed ashore by a tsunami. Andy found one sailboat that looked salvageable. *Maybe sail it to the other Islands. Find life.* That became the plan.

After setting up a compound near the harbor, the family began work on the boat. A month later, Andy and Eddie set sail for the other islands. They returned in two weeks. Alone. Andy shook his head.

"Nothing."

After a week of the blues, Doc and Carla thought it time for a family pow-wow. They had been thinking for a while about their future and decided this was a good time to share. "What if we *are* the only people left?" Doc asked, "But so what? We know how to survive. We don't need money. We have no bills to pay. No pollution. No traffic. No politics. No crime. No war. We can grow veggies and fruit, catch fish, and stay warm."

Carla chipped in, "And what's the worst that can happen to us here? A volcano? An earthquake? Ha! Bring it. We've survived a nuclear war and an asteroid drive-by. People would kill to live here." And so, it was.

As the years went by, the family did grow. First it was Sara and Andy producing a baby girl. A year later, a baby boy. Then it was Casey and Jenny proliferating, followed closely by Eddie and Laura. The first family now numbered sixteen. Wildlife began to appear. Birds flew, butterflies flitted. Life was promising. Nonetheless, a couple of things still puzzled Doc; the seasons, such as they were, seemed to be lasting longer than before. The moon looked different too. After a year of monitoring such things, Doc was convinced that Earth was taking longer to orbit the sun. Then it dawned on him; he had not been wrong about the asteroid's trajectory after all.

Earth had rocked itself so hard with nuclear bombs that *it* was now in a new orbit. By Doc's count there were now 372 days in a year. Overall temperatures had cooled somewhat. Climate change was changing...back.

Every day for the next 12 years Doc started his day out by scanning the horizon with binoculars. Finding nothing, he resumed tending his garden. One morning a spot appeared on the horizon. The family quickly gathered on the lookout point and lit a signal fire. Through the glasses Doc saw a large sailboat. Its mainsail was ripped and the boat appeared to be struggling to stay afloat. On deck, furry humanoid-like creatures seemed to be arguing and fighting while raising a flag of some sort. Doc turned away and looked back at his Eden.

"Andy, do you remember where we put those guns we had?"

.

AN ADVENTURE AWAITS YOU IN

LESSONS LEARNT

TERRY CUBBINS

LESSONS LEARNED

It seemed like it took forever to eliminate the virus, but, in the end, the war was won. Those who were most instrumental in conquering the epidemic did so by studying history. They looked back on the Black Plaque, the Hantavirus, Ebola, Rabies, HIV, Malaria, the Swine Flu and others. Those in charge learned what went wrong in the past. Armed with this information, they decided to put everything they had into the Coronavirus. They felt they had no choice. It was now or never.

It was touch and go for a while, but perseverance paid off. They were finally able to wipe the virus off the face of the Earth. And when they did, the planet began to recover. The quality of the air improved dramatically. Streams, lakes and oceans began trending pollution free. Foliage returned in abundance, enough to feed the planet.

There was quiet. Yes, it took ages for bats, rats,

chickens and pigs, monkeys, mosquitoes and a host of others to finally eliminate the disease that the Animal Kingdom knew as…the Humanoid Virus.

AN ADVENTURE AWAITS YOU IN

THE EMPEROR'S NEW HAIR

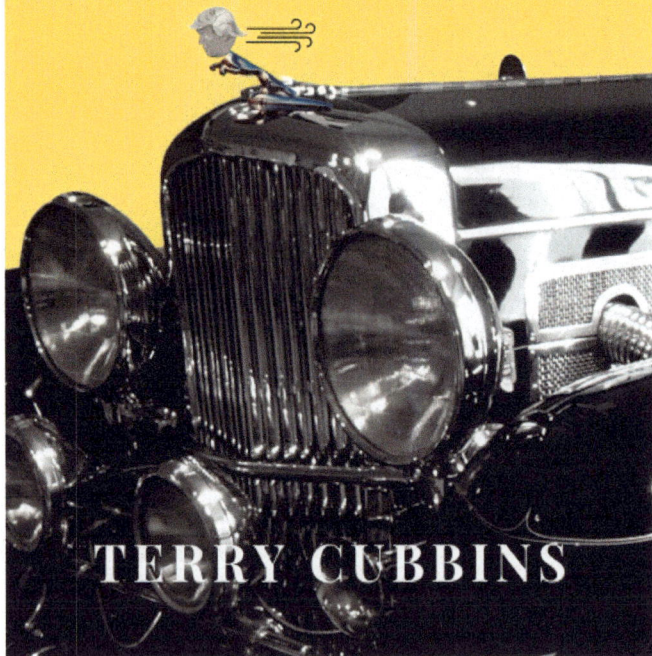

TERRY CUBBINS

THE EMPEROR'S NEW HAIR

Ronald Von Frump was born in a small European country in June of 1946 with a silver spoon in his mouth. The spoon was courtesy of Ronald's father, Frederick King Frump. Frederick (Fred) Frump was one of the richest men in the land, having made his fortune selling modular castles and knock-off diamonds to unsuspecting immigrants and Flemish people during the 1930's.

The Frumps lived in a 10,000 square-foot; 12-room modular castle perched on a hilltop just outside of town. Ronald 's mother, Lady Ronda, as she was known by, but only by herself, claimed to be a distant relative of King Leopold I who ruled Belgium in 1831. Because of this perceived tie to a monarchy, Lady Ronda never saw the need to cook, drive, or change the diaper of her only child. She did however, have the wherewithal to hire a nanny, chef and chauffeur to serve the family.

Up until he was about four-years old, Ronald believed he had been born into a royal family and would one day be King of all the land. When his father explained to him that they lived in a Democratic society and not one of a Monarchy, he was shocked to learn that he was not in line for any kind of throne. His father even went as far as to explain what a democracy was using Churchill's assessment, 'Democracy is the worst form of government, except for all the others.'

Not to be deterred, Ronald, or, as he would sometimes later be known as, 'The Ronald,' 'Ron-Ron,' or, 'His Ronald-ness,' pressed on as a child of privilege. One day he overheard his playmates talking about him and the silver spoon thing. Young Ronald immediately began raging, informing everybody within shouting distance that the story was fake news, a hoax - a total witch-hunt. The truth, he said, was that the spoon was not silver at all, it was 14 carat gold.

At five years of age, Ronald was receiving an allowance of 50 francs a week. His account was handled mostly by his nanny, Bridget Peeters. Peeters was a sweet, twenty-one- year-old, blue-eyed blonde. Despite these handicaps, she was a conscientious, hardworking young lady who was putting herself through college with hopes of earning a teaching degree.

To make sure that Ronald would grow up like any other normal child, the Frumps enrolled him in a semi-private school with girls and everything. It was there that Ronald V. Frump truly learned the value of his family name. He was a Frump. That alone entitled him to good grades. Once, when Ronald was still in his early ten's, a teacher had the audacity to tell his parents that he wasn't doing well in school and bullying other kids. That teacher was soon flipping patties in Hamburg, Germany. Ronald knew he was a star at an early age. He could grab a girl by her pigtail anytime he wanted and get away with it. If he had to, he could always buy off his victims with his allowance money. As he grew older, The Ronald moved up to bigger and better things, like trying to cop a feel from nanny Peeters whenever he could.

When Ronald turned fourteen, his father summoned him to his office for a little father-to-son business talk. "Someday son, all of this will be yours." Fred Frump said. To seem interested and to counteract the yawn that was forming, Ronald allowed his mind to drift toward his future; beautiful girls… jealous friends…cool cars…. a private golf club with women rub-downers, swimming pool, more girls. Power. Fame. Getting his picture taken… Ronnie's reverie was broken when his father rolled on. "With that in mind, son, I feel it's time for you to experience the dignity of labor as well as money management. That's why starting next week, after school, I've arranged for you to take a job."

Ronald coughed. "A what?"

"That's right, son, a job. A paper route. Just like your little friends have."

Ronald thought that paper routes were for losers

who didn't have girlfriends. Although he hadn't put a move on Lila Flect at school yet, he was planning to. A paper-route? He wouldn't get halfway down the foul line with Lila Flect if she knew he had a paper-route. However, Fred Frump was adamant about his plan and dismissed his son, saying "Congratulations, Ron-Ron, you'll soon be gainfully employed."

Ronald pouted for a couple of days and then came up with a solution for his dilemma. The day before he was to start his route, he limped into the nurse's office at school complaining of foot pain. It took some convincing and a small percent of his allowance but Ronald came away with what he felt he needed. Armed with a note from the nurse describing his unfortunate case of bone spurs, Ronald confronted his father with the sad news. Fred frowned, didn't say anything for a moment, but then snapped his fingers. "Wait. I know how badly you want this job, son. So, I'll have Earl drive you to your appointed rounds."

Ronald wasted no time going straight to Earl and

explaining how this relationship was going to work. Soon enough, Earl was tossing the newspapers while His Ronaldness was making out with Lila in the backseat of the limo.

Not long after Ronald turned 16, Fred Frump instructed Peeters to teach his son how to drive a car. She was to use her own vehicle, a Volkswagen Beetle, and find a lonely stretch of road before she put Ronald behind the wheel. The first thing Ronald did when he got behind the wheel was to pop the clutch and stall the motor. After a couple of bucks and lurches he finally got the Bug rolling forward. When he reached 9 km/h it was time to shift gears. Ronald again struggled until Peeters leaned over from the passenger's seat and helped him find second. In doing so, Peeters exposed some cleavage while allowing her scent to float over him. It took Ronald several tries before he was able to engage second gear successfully. Third and fourth gear was more of the same. Finally, they came to a turnout on the road and Peeters, said, "Pull over here and stop. Maybe we should practice parking for a while."

Whoa, wrong thing to say.

As soon as the car jerked to a stop, Ronald practically jumped over the gearshift and started groping Peeters. Peeters, who had already caught Ronald playing with himself several times and knew that he was still wetting the bed, tried to push him away. Peeters squirmed and swatted at Ronald but he persisted. Then, just as quickly as it all began, Ronnie made an 'ugggahh' sound and collapsed across Peeters. She thought that maybe she had hit him in the eye or something. But when she pushed him away, she saw the wet spot on his pants. Then she did something that she probably shouldn't have; she burst out laughing.

Later that evening, as the Frump family gathered for dinner, Lady Ronda asked, "How did your driving lesson go, dear?"

Ronald shrugged. "Okay, I guess."

"Just, okay? Care to elaborate, son?"

"Well, I really don't want to get Ms. Peeters in

trouble, but she was cross with me and cursed when I missed a shift once."

Frederick (Fred) King Frump and Lady Ronda looked at each other. The next morning, Peeters was sent packing. At the tender age of 16 and a quarter, The Ronald was suddenly nanny-less.

As Ronald approached his eighteenth birthday and about to enter college, Fred Frump could sense that his son had yet to experience the world of man-dom. Fred took it upon himself to help matters along by enlisting the help of his own masseuse and hair stylist, Ginger Duwright. Surreptitiously as a birthday present, Fred presented his son with a gift certificate to Duwright's salon on the far side of town. "Here, son. Happy Birthday. It's time to let a professional do you...your hair, I mean."

As soon as Ronald stepped into Duwright's salon, he was met by Ginger. She was about thirty-years old, long brown hair, dark brown eyes, and very pretty. She wore a short black skirt with an off-the-shoulders white peasant blouse that she filled out nicely. She smiled, bowed slightly and motioned Reggie into her salon. As he stepped forward, Ronald heard the door lock behind him and the sound of venetian blinds being lowered. Silently, Ginger took Ronald's hand and led him across a lush red carpet to a single barber's style chair on the far side of the room. The entire salon featured wall-to-wall-to-ceiling mirrors. There were no other stylists or customers in sight.

Once Ronald was comfortably seated, Ginger assumed a professional stance in front of him, examining his hair, touching it here and there. She placed one hand on his jaw and moved his head from side to side. Then she stood on her toes and leaned in, ostensibly to study the top of his head. The movement brought her breasts up to within blinking distance of Ron's right eye. Finally, she stood back and looked at him. "You have such beautiful hair, but …would you mind terribly if we try a different look for you?" She took his head in her hands and drilled her eyes into his. "Something that says…POWER, you know?"

Ronald liked the idea. "Yes," he gulped.

Ginger mussed and fussed with his hair for the next forty-five minutes, somehow keeping her breasts within inches of his face the entire time.

Finally, after spraying his hair with a special liquid-cement quick-set, Ginger pivoted the chair around so that her new client could see the mirror. "Behold," she said. "Is that a work of art or what?"

Ronald's hair was now shaped like a 1935 Duesenberg hood ornament, and before he could say anything, Ginger spun him back around, leaned in and looked deep into his eyes.

"Now, you now have the power sir. Women everywhere will not be able to resist you." To prove her point, she whipped the cover off of Ronald, unzipped his trousers, dropped her skirt and mounted him. This time like a true cowboy, Ronald managed to hold on for the eight second ride.

Later, as Ginger savored a cigarette, she suggested to Ronald that he come in for a weekly trim and set. "To keep the look balanced and fresh," she said. She also let him know that she wouldn't be charging him for his visits as his new hair style would be a walking advertisement for her business. "Quid por quo, you know?"

Ronald couldn't understand why someone would trade squid for crow, but if that's what she wanted it was fine by him.

The next four years Ronald went to college and spent his time pointing his hair at women. When he did bother to learn something, it was that the new math they were teaching in this handpicked school was exactly what he needed to earn his B.S. degree in business b.s. It was a complicated formula but, in the end, it proved that mediocrity, when interpreted properly, can result in glowing grades for certain people. It also helps when the president of the college is a longtime pal of the Frump Family.

Besides women, another thing that Ronald picked up while in college was golf. He found he could move and shake better on the golf course rather than in a classroom. It's where he learned the 'Art of the Deal,' aka, how to sandbag, inflate, or deflate a golf handicap as needed, or cheating, if you will.

After college Ronald entered into the work force by applying for a job with the Frump Kastle Company. Not only did he get the job, he got the company. But, before Frederick would hand over the keys to the corporation, he strongly urged his son to get married. "I'd be pleased if you had a son, son. We need to carry on the Frump name, you know."

The name didn't require too much heavy lifting at the time, but before The Ronald would be through, the name Frump would be seen everywhere. Ronald dutifully took a wife and instructed her to have a son. He had so much fun trying to make a son that when he finally did have one, he told his wife, whose name was Irene, "Let's have another one." After slipping a daughter in there, they had another son for backup.

The first couple of years in the business world

went okay for The Ronald. Mostly because he was spending more time on the golf course then he was at the office. It wasn't long however, that he noticed that his subordinates at his company were getting their pictures in the business section of the Daily Planet Newspaper while nothing much was being said about his leadership. One newspaper reporter, a young man named Olson Jamison, went on to predict continued success for the company as long as Ronald stayed the course. It didn't take much imagination to guess which course he was referring to.

Ronald continued to play golf every morning, but limited it to nine holes so he could hurry to the office, check his hair, sit in his captains' chair and keep a lookout for reporters with cameras.

With nothing much else to do, Ronald tinkered around his office until he stumbled onto some of his business's financial statements. Applying his B.S. in new math, he soon came up with an idea that would increase profits even more, surely leading to his picture in the paper. A big part of his plan was centered on a tax maneuver that he had just invented.

Six months later, Ronald did get his picture in the paper, accompanied by the banner, "Ronald Von Frump, Bankrupt!"

Ronnie immediately explained to his father how it wasn't his fault. It was the jealous, near-sighted comptroller, who bungled the finances of the company. "It's sad. I didn't really know her," he said.

Father bailed out son and son quickly set out to re-make his fortune, this time in the entertainment and gambling industry. Ronald built a lavish casino that looked like it might be a winner for a while, but he got himself in trouble again by reneging on bonuses due to contractors who built the place. This resulted in fines and penalties that forced Ronald to refinance at a much higher interest rate than the original bank note. After that, he was able to stay afloat for a couple of years, giving him a chance to build even more things to put his name on, but, eventually, this insatiable desire to stamp Frump on everything led him to bankruptcy court again.

This time his father wasn't around to bail his son out, having suffered an untimely death, (vs a timely death,) from pneumonia just before Ronald's second tumble from grace. A few months later, Lady Ronda checked out as well. There was a will, of course, which helped, but not as much as The Ronald was counting on.

It was during his second go-round in the courts that Ronald discovered how bankruptcy laws could actually benefit him personally in the future. He saw how he could manipulate certain parts of the laws to provide himself with a virtual parachute, if and when he ran another company off a cliff.

He proved his theory by going bankrupt every so often, leaving investors out to dry, while he would emerge from the bankruptcy unscathed. After a short period of required dust settling he would then play the game again. He would raise the bar higher, borrow more than he had ever before and start up another company, all without the fear of failing or losing any of his personal finances. Nevertheless, there was one thing that did fail about this time; his marriage. Irene had had enough of the rollercoaster life. She packed her bags, grabbed the kids, and flew the king dome. She claimed it was because of his cheating, although she didn't narrow it down to which arena or what form.

Ronald knew that the failed marriage was not his fault and vowed that if he ever got married again, he would insist on a prenuptial; his next wife would get only a fraction of his worth and it would be mandatory she take custody of any pets that might be involved.

As time rolled on, Ronald blew through another marriage and a couple more businesses, all while keeping his hair perfectly coiffed. Because of this trait of keeping his hair in place and always landing on his feet, no matter who he ran over, Ronald began to pick up a following. Some sleepy people liked his bullish style, while those who were paying attention, not so much. One of the not-so-mucher's was reporter Olson Jamison, who was now chronicling Ronald's escapades on a regular basis. Examples of Ronnie's mounting failures were easy to come by. Besides the number of casinos and hotels, there was Frump Airlines, Frump Colognes, Frump University, Frump Mattress, Frump Vodka, a board game in his name, he even tried his brand on Frump Steaks, but with so much bull involved, it went under as well. Surprisingly, he never sought to promote a hair cement product; maybe thinking it was his little secret.

However, Ronald never stopped looking for a new angle and when he noticed that the Pope was getting a lot of press, he wondered if there might be money in religion. Being the mercenary that he was, Ronald figured he could take up whatever faith was selling best and work an angle. But when the Pope heard about some of Ronald's shenanigans, he suggested a moral course for him. The Ronald, in his ever-diplomatic way, fired back at the Pope, saying, "Go back to Popeing and mind your own business."

The closest Ronald ever got to religion was when he formed a charity foundation in his name. When he was later caught stealing money from the charity and putting into his own personal account, that little enterprise went kaput too.

As he grew older, Ronald hardly slowed down at all, mostly because he wanted his name on as many things as possible while he could still breathe. A few of his disciples had suggested politics for him but he had always felt that public service was beneath him. But then it hit him; he was not in-line for any throne or anything, so why not politics? Not the lower echelon crap, like a mayor or governor, but why not be president of a country? Other people would put his name on things for him. He imagined airports, highways, and aircraft carriers. There would be statues and museums. The Nobel Peace Prize would likely be re-named, *The Frump Piece Prize*. People would worship him and in the end, that's what he sought most of all.

So, at an age when most people are retired or dead, Ronald tossed his hat in as a presidential candidate.

Having no previous political experience, he ran on the, 'I'm a genius platform,' which in his mind meant he'd figure stuff out by his own self.

During his campaign, while his opponents bantered back and forth about the usual social, domestic and economic issues, Ronald boasted that after he won the election, he would make all of the rest of the countries in the world pay-up and behave, or else.

Fortunately for Ronald, his run for the presidency came while most of the country was sick of politics or asleep. And even though the majority of the people voted for his opponent, one morning the people of the country woke up to find The Ronald as their president.

Ronald started his presidency rolling by claiming a record-sized crowd for the inauguration. Then he insisted it was voter fraud that kept him from winning the popular vote. The economy was really good now because God wanted him to be president. "No other president has done more for religion than me." This was most likely true as people who had never prayed before, began to.

As far as all the women who were accusing him of sexual misconduct, he professed that he had never even met most of them and they were all lying. He also said that his tax returns were forth coming.

As all of this continued to spew out of his mouth, his political opposition party began looking closer at him. Ronald immediately went on the attack claiming it was all just a witch-hunt, a hoax, an attempt to overthrow his government. He had already declared himself to be the best president the country ever had and would ever have.

As more accusations and past misdeeds came to light, reporter Olson Jamison kept reporting. Jamison had somehow found out about Ronald's earlier bone spurs claim and suggested that the condition had morphed into *brain spurs* for the President. This really pissed The Ronald off. He declared the newspaper to be an enemy of the State and that Olson was a traitor and should be hanged. Ronald went so far as to have Olson secretly investigated in hopes he could find dirt on him and expose him for the 'Never Frump,' dirty coward that he was.

The investigation didn't turn up any dirt on Olson, but it did show that Olson was now engaged to Ronald's former nanny, Bridget Peeters. Peeters of course, could supply a ton of embarrassing dirt on The Ronald if she chose to.

Ronald quickly instructed his personal attorney, Rollie Jockanoff, to get both Olson and Peeters, shipped back to where they came from. When told that they both came from his country, His Ronald-ness ordered them back to the shit-hole country where they should have come from.

Rollie knew how to get these types of things done

while keeping his distance from the thugs who did the actual shipping. "Don't tell me how you do it," he told his associates, "Just do it." It wasn't long before Olson and Peeters seemed to vanish.

Then, after years of bullying and insulting people, some pesky periodicals and newscasts showed Ronald Von Frump, slipping in the polls. "Polls are rigged," he said, "They're scams."

With less than a year to go in his first term, his political foes began to look at possible impeachment for, *'obstruction of just about everything.'*

Ronald knew that to ensure his legacy he would most certainly have to avoid impeachment and win the next election. Visions of boulevards in his name, minted coins with his profile on them, the monuments, parks, mountains, maybe even the country would be renamed in his honor, it all suddenly seemed to be in jeopardy.

Ronald huddled with Rollie again to look for a

stratagem.

*   *   *

Six months later

On a tiny, remote island near the island of Borneo where they had been banished to, Olson Jamison and Bridget Peeters were in their hut having their morning coffee and getting ready for work. Bridget was employed part time as a maid at the only hotel on the island and Olson was on assignment from the Bruni Gazette to study the mating habits of the Flying Box Bat. Both of their commutes were short. Bridget's took her just under one minute to walk the two hundred yards from their beach hut to the one-star, two- story hotel with four rooms.

Olson's commute took him just a shade longer as he had to walk to the jungle's edge, which was about a five-iron away. As they were finishing their coffee, Peeter's co-worker Mirza, who had just returned by boat from visiting her sister in Bruni, stuck her head into the hut and announced matter-of-factly, "You President. He dead."

"Yeah, well, good morning to you too," Peeters said, "What president? What are you talking about? Come in here."

Marzi stepped in and bowed slightly. "Yes. I see news in Bruni. President Mister Frump. He die. He run into building on fire. Try to save people. Maybe save dog, too. You not know?"

Peeters shot Olson a look. "Know?! How could we know anything living here?" Peeters moaned. "There's noooo thing here. No phones, no pools, no pets, you know?"

Mirza was no longer looking smug and was beginning to tear up. Peeters immediately put her arm around her co-worker. "I'm sorry, Mirza. Its… it's just that, I'm, well, you know, I'm terribly upset by the news. President Frump is dead?"

Peeters looked over Mariz's shoulder at Olson who winked back at her. Peeters and Olson both knew that Mariz didn't always have all the facts in the right order, so, after a few 'thank you's for telling us',

Peeters gently turned Marzi back toward the huts entry flap.

After Marzi left, Olson was the first to say, "Ronald Von Frump running into a burning building? To save a dog? I don't think so. Who we talkin' about here?"

"Exactly," Bridget said.

"But, if something did happen," Olson said. "Maybe those two old rabbi-looking guys I saw checking in to the hotel last week know something?"

"I doubt it," Peeters said. "They asked me not to bother them. I think they're fasting or something."

They mulled it over some more before deciding to take Marzi's information with a grain of salt. In the meantime, they'd just have wait for the next boat from the mainland for any news.

That afternoon, Peeters and Olson set out on a trail in the jungle to wander and ponder. Olson, as usual had his camcorder with him in the event they ever spotted a Flying Box Bat. The joke between them was if they ever did see a bat in the daytime, it was probably blind as one and didn't know it was daylight.

They followed the trail that would lead them back to the beach at some point. An hour later, hot and sweaty, they came to the spot where they would usually strip down, dash from the jungle to the ocean for a swim and then rest in the shade before heading back. This time however, after their swim, lovemaking preceded casual rest, which in turn, resulted in real rest.

Peeters was dozing with her head on Olson's chest when she heard voices. At first, she thought it was part of a dream or something. She sat up and covered her breasts. Peeking through the foliage to the beach, she saw the two guests from the hotel approaching. Their white robes and sandals set off nicely by long, dark beards and black, matador-looking type hats.

Olson began to stir. He opened one eye and asked, "What's goin'on hon?"

"Sssshh..." she whispered. "The two guys from the

hotel are coming down the beach."

Olson sat up. "Oh, good," he said. "Let's go ask them if---"

"Wait silly, we're naked."

"So? I'm sure---"

"Oh my God. They're coming this way. Get down!"

Olson and Peeters crouched down and watched as the two men approached the edge of the jungle. They were close enough now that they could hear what the men were saying.

"At least the lunch was good," the taller of the two said. "Some kind of bird?"

"Yes,' the shorter one said. "It was the Rhinoceros Hornbill. They're endangered."

"That explains it," taller guy said. "Endangered always tastes better."

They took a couple of steps before the tall one stopped and bent down to adjust one of his sandals. "I don't know why they call these goddamn things sandals," he said. "They're not worth a shit in this sand."

"Your bone spurs acting up again, sir?" his companion asked.

Taller guy smirked and said, "Yeah right counselor." He took another step but his sandal came loose again. "Hey, I gotta sit down for a minute." He limped over to a log not twenty feet from where Olson and Bridget sat stunned, watching and listening. When the other man sat down on the log next to his buddy, Peeters looked at Olson, pointed to his camcorder and made a spinning motion with her finger.

As the two men sat on the log looking out at the ocean, taller guy said, "I don't know why we had to come to this godforsaken place. There's no phone, no internet or television, not even any women to grab or look at."

"Hey! Everything worked out, right?" his buddy said. "The building fire, the explosion, the diversion. All there, right?"

"Yeah. Well, don't forget it was me that put in a tunnel leading away from my building," tall guy said.

"I thought it might come in handy someday." He paused, then said, "But damnit, I'm missing everything. I don't even get to see the flags at half-mast or anything. And I cut my hair off for Christ sakes! My hair!" Then, he stood up, tugged on his beard, and added, "And if cutting my hair off wasn't bad enough, now I gotta put up with this damn thing." As he spoke, he lifted a fake beard away from his face and rubbed his jaw. Olson's and Peeters jaws dropped even further has the camcorder silently rolled on.

Taller guy's friend said, "Well, you'll only be here until your real beard grows out and we know that they've found your official will and have read it," his friend said.

"You have any idea how much my hair coulda' been worth?" Taller guy fussed his beard back in place and said, "Oh, well, I gotta tell you, Rollie, leaving stuff to the local children's hospitals and the humane society in my will was a nice touch. They'll probably declare a holiday in my name just for that. But, what about my off-shore accounts?"

"All there. All accounted for," Rollie replied.

"Nice work."

"Yeah, well that's what us lawyers are for."

Then taller guy got up and took a step and turned toward Olson and Bridget. He fumbled around in the front of his robe for several seconds before finally finding what he was searching for. He pried the little thing out, farted and began peeing with it. He looked back over his shoulder at his pal and said, "I hope my kids understand why I didn't leave them very much. They need to earn everything for themselves you know, like I did. I think my wife will be fine, too. There's not many people who own a 4'x8' portrait of me."

Olson kept filming as the two men gathered themselves and started back down the beach toward the hotel.

As they walked away, taller guy said, "Well, Rollie, you and I are the only ones in the world who know about this. I think I can safely say that my legacy is now assured."

"Yes, Mr. President," Rollie answered. "If your place in history isn't secured by now, it soon will be."

Written in 2018

AN ADVENTURE AWAITS YOU IN

SO...? HELP ME GOD!

TERRY CUBBINS

SO...? HELP ME GOD!

Sara Erskine had never been in a courtroom in her life let alone being on trial for capital murder. When she was first called to the witness stand her immediate impression of it was that it was very uncomfortable. Not the stand part, but the chair itself. Made of polished oak and tilted slightly forward just enough that when she sat on it, she slipped forward and her skirt inched up. She had to grab the armrests to push herself back up and then replanted her feet and sat ramrod straight. Crossing her legs would be out of the question. Even the armrests seemed to be higher than needed, making her feel somewhat smaller than she already was, especially with Judge Delridge looking down on her from his lofted perch, a statue of Lady Justice back-dropping him. The thought crossed her mind that nobody sits above the law. Even in today's world, Sara certainly didn't look like the type of woman that would purposely shoot her husband in the chest from point blank range. The man she was accused of murdering was Charlie Philip

Erskine, her husband of eighteen months. Charlie wasn't bad to look at if you like your Charlies' with a little sheen to them. Black hair combed straight back, dark brown eyes, mischievous grin, that sort of thing. Sara said the shooting was an accident, but the State was saying otherwise.

Sara was twenty-four years old, stood 5' 3", and weighed barely a hundred pounds. She had light brown hair that she usually wore in a ponytail when she wasn't on trial for murder. Today she wore her hair loosely down to her shoulders which helped frame a beguiling face featuring hazel-colored eyes, soft, clear skin and a hint of dimples which in normal conditions punctuated a bright smile. She could've been the girl next door; the one that every father hoped his son would marry. She was polite, got good grades in school, somewhat shy, and unaware of her natural beauty. Loved animals. Good at sports, especially golf and tennis.

Tragically, just before Sara graduated college, her

parents were killed in a freak accident aboard a cruise ship when the glass- encased elevator they were riding in inexplicitly jolted to a stop, blowing out a glass panel and the handrail they were holding on to. The couple fell seven stories to the atrium deck below. The resulting lawsuit was substantial; leaving Sara set for life as far as money was concerned. Enough money to hire a good lawyer for her trial if she was so inclined. However, the lawyer she hired was her only remaining relative, her uncle, Wally Clifford. Wally was more of an ambulance-chaser-type attorney and had never taken part in a serious trial before. When the State offered to reduce the charge to Involuntary Manslaughter, Sara rejected the plea saying, "Uncle Wally is family and he knows I'm telling the truth when I say the shooting was an accident."

Uncle Wally was 46 years old, a divorced father of none, somewhat paunchy, wore suspenders and a belt just to be safe. His comb-over didn't require a full-toothed comb, yet the hair from his back invaded his shoulders and neck. He wore thick glasses that magnified the size of his brown eyeballs by four times when he looked straight at you. Basically though, Wally was a good guy who just didn't care to spend a lot of time in front of a mirror. Wally also appeared to be unaware of the basic rule of thumb (especially in murder trials) that it was usually a bad decision to let your client take the stand.

The first question directed at Sara as she sat in the witness chair, came from the State's prosecutor, Edward Tolby. Tolby, who looked enough like former National Security Advisor, John Bolton, to play him in the upcoming movie, approached her and began.

"Mrs. Erskine, you've already admitted shooting your husband on the night of June seventeenth while you were in the study of your apartment, but for the sake of clarity, I'd like to provide the jury with a chronological version of events that led up to that night. Could you please tell the court how you met your husband, the late Charlie Erskine?"

Sara took a breath and began. "Yes, well, I first met Charlie at the Dakota Cafe, downtown on Fourth

Avenue where he worked. I was having lunch with my friend, Collette." Sara smiled at her friend who had already testified in court and was sitting in the gallery.

"We liked to meet up there for lunch on Fridays."

"What was your husbands' station at the cafe?"

"Station?"

"Yes. What did he do there?"

"Oh, sure. Well, he was, uh, you know, bussing tables I guess you'd call it. But he was only doing that until he could get his book published, you see, he---"

"So, he came to your table? Took your dishes away?"

"Yes, I think so, but I didn't really notice him then. It was later when I went to pay for lunch, it was my turn to pay, because Collette ---"

"You went to pay, and then what happened?"

"Well, I couldn't find my wallet. I kept digging around in my purse, I was starting to panic."

"Go on."

"Well, that's when Charlie tapped me on the shoulder. He said, 'Excuse, miss, I think you may have dropped this,' or something like that. He handed me my wallet. God, I was so embarrassed, but really, really grateful. I thanked him of course. I…I tried to give him a tip but he wouldn't take it. He bowed just a little, kinda like the Japanese do, you know? Said he had to get back to work."

"Was there anything missing from your wallet?"

"Oh, no. Nothing."

"When did you see him again?"

"The next Friday when Collette and I had lunch at the Café. We were a little later than usual and there wasn't much of a crowd, in fact Charlie was on a break sitting at a table by himself, writing something. Working on his manuscript I guess. Anyway, Collette saw him first, she thought Charlie was pretty hot, not that she would do anything of course, she's married and all." Again, Sara sneaked a peek and at her friend.

"Anyway, she told me I should go over and say hi, you know, thank him again. It was after that that Charlie and I started seeing each other."

"What was your courtship like? Dinner? Movies?"

"Well, not so much. Charlie didn't have a lot of money saved or anything and he said he didn't feel right about going out too much until he could afford to pay his way. Said it would be about six months before he would be able to get his book published, and then he'd be able to get a nicer apartment, maybe even buy a car. In the meantime, we'd take rides out of the city in my car. Have picnics. Take walks. That sorta stuff. Or, we'd watch movies at my place and I would fix dinner. Charlie said I was a fantastic cook. He said I should write a book. A cookbook."

"What about his book? What was he working on?"

Sara shrugged. "I thought at the time it was a murder mystery of some sort. Charlie said it was bad luck to talk about it or even show me anything until it was done."

Tolby nodded, like that made sense. "And how long did the two of you date before you were married?"

"A couple of months, I guess."

"Kind of a whirlwind romance then, huh?"

"Objection," Walley yelled. "Irrelevant!"

Judge Erskine peered over his bifocals at Wally.

"No need to shout, counselor, we can all hear you."

Before Erskine could rule on Wally's objection, Tolby jumped in; "Your Honor, I'm merely trying to add another building block of evidence for a motive in this case which will be made clear very soon."

"Very well. Objection overruled. You may continue."

Tolby thumbed both sides of his mustache and then asked Sara, "Is it safe to assume that while you were dating, you two were happy? No arguments? No disagreements?"

"Oh, no, we were very happy."

"Whose idea was to get married? Yours or Mr. Erskine's?"

"Well, mostly mine," Sara said. "Charlie wanted to wait until after his book was finished before we got married."

"Mrs. Erskine, your friend, Collette Pruh, has already testified that not long after you were married, you called her on several occasions to discuss your marriage. Isn't it true, that during those calls, you confided in your friend that there were some things that your husband was doing that were becoming irritating? And that you were having disagreements?"

"Yes, but I suppose all marriages have some---"

"Tell us Mrs. Erskine, specifically, what some of these annoyances were, and remember, besides your friend's testimony, you swore on the bible to tell the truth, so help you God."

Sara glanced at Collette who was sitting in the gallery, then: "Well…Charlie started leaving his clothes on the floor, like in the bedroom and bathroom. He never did that before." Sara blushed, and added; "He…he was leaving the toilet seat up, too."

As Tolby nodded and checked his notes, Sara continued. "But we never really had any big arguments, or fights, more like disagreements. Like, once when we were watching a Brad Pitt movie, I told Charlie how much I liked him, Brad Pitt, I mean.

Charlie said that he thought Brad Pitt was over-rated and not even that good-looking. Then he just got up and went to bed. See? Silly stuff like that."

"What else, Mrs. Erskine?" Tolby asked. "What other things about your husbands' manners or behavior did you begin to find irritating?"

"I dunno, but it seemed like the times we did go out he would talk louder than he needed to, like at dinner or a movie? He just wasn't used to going out."

"Your friend, Collette testified about an incident golf course. Would you tell us about that?"

"Okay, once, when Charlie and I were playing golf with Collette and her husband, Jason, Charlie was having trouble getting out of a sand trap and he threw his club. It hit Collette in the shin. I think it was more of a slip, though, accidental, you know?"

Tolby let that statement settle in, then; "Isn't it also true that you thought Charlie's driving habits had changed as well? Not with a golf club, I mean, when he was driving a car. Your car."

Sara sighed and then nodded, "Yeah, I guess so. When we were dating, Charlie was a good driver. I felt safe. But then, one day on the interstate, he began driving too fast, changing lanes all over the place and tailgating other cars, you know, following too close?"

"Yes, Mrs. Erskine. Go on. Did you say something to him about it?"

"Yes, I asked him to slow down a little."

"And? "

"Well, he got kinda mad. Swore a little. I think traffic can get on anybody's nerves though. You know---"

"What did he do then?"

"He slowed way down, moved into the left lane and stayed there."

"Left lane?" Tolby paused and sauntered over to the jury box which consisted of seven women and five men. He made eye contact with every one of them before he turned back to Sara.

"Alright Mrs. Erskine, thank you for that. Now, if you will, please take us back to the night you shot your husband and tell us exactly what you were doing before he arrived home that evening."

Sara sniffled once. "Well, Charlie always wanted

dinner ready when he got home, which was usually around seven o'clock, so I had put a pork roast in the oven earlier."

"When your husband didn't arrive by seven, what did you do?"

"I called him."

"Did you talk with him?"

"No, it went to recording, so I left a message for him to call me."

"Were you concerned or… angry?"

"I…I was worried. He really hadn't been himself lately. I think he was having writer's block or whatever you call it."

"You say you had noticed a difference in his behavior. Did that extend to the bedroom?"

"Objecti---!"

"Overruled. Please answer the question, Mrs. Erskine."

Sara swallowed hard and looked down at her lap again. When she looked up again tears silently rolled down her cheeks as she answered. "Well, we hadn't, uh, you know, made love in a while, if that's what you mean. Charlie had a lot on his mind, trying to get published. I don't think he wanted to admit that he couldn't, you know…?"

"Couldn't? Or wouldn't, Mrs. Erskine?"

"Oh, god! What difference does it make?" Sara was sobbing now.

Tolby gave her time to collect herself, then; "Okay, back to the night in question. After you left your husband a message to call you, what happened then?"

"Well, just as I was taking the roast out of the oven, my phone rang. It was lying on the counter and I could see that the number was Charlie's. I tried to set the roast down in a hurry but my hand slipped off of the mitten and I burned my fingers."

Sara looked down at the palm of her left hand. "It was really hurting so I went into the bathroom and put some salve on it. Then I went back into the kitchen to see if Charlie had left a message."

"Was there a message, Mrs. Erskine?"

"Yes."

"But it wasn't from Charlie was it, Mrs. Erskine?"

"No."

"Your Honor, at this time the prosecution would like to introduce exhibit B to the court. It is Mrs. Erskine's cellphone with a recording of the phone call, taken from Mrs. Erskine's voicemail."

Wally mindlessly tugged at his right suspender strap while staring at nothing.

Tolby approached the bench and handed the phone to Judge Delridge. Delridge gave it a once-over before motioning to the court clerk. The clerk approached the bench, took the handoff from the judge and walked the phone back to his desk where he had a small, black speaker set up. He plugged the phone into the speaker, then stood, waiting further instructions.

The courtroom was dead quiet for several seconds, then like an executioner, Judge Delridge nodded to the clerk and the recording began. A woman's voice in a nasal Bronxsy twang suddenly filled the courtroom.

"Hey, Sara? ... Hey, listen, you don't know me but I thought

you outta know a few things about your hubby. For one thing, he's gonna be a little late for dinner, he's not dressed yet. In fact, he's still naked."

The voice coughed a couple of times, *"'Scues me, gawd, I gotta quit this smokin' shit. But hey, you know how it is, gotta have a cigarette after sex right hon? Anyhows, your Chucky's in the shower right now so's I thought I'd clue you in how he's been playing you. Just like he's been playin' me, cept, I'm gonna bail on his sorry ass 'cause I just heard from another babe who he's been playin' too. She enlightened me, so's I'm enlighten' you, know what I'm sayin'? You've been set up here, dearie. The only reason Charlie married you was to get some of that dough you got. He knew about your inheritance. It was in the papers. Parents killed like that? That was a big story. He picked your pocket lady, literally and figuratively, no shit. You know about Charlies' sheet, right? A rap sheet is what I'm talkin' here. Mostly petty stuff, but still… Anyhow's, the plan was to get you to marry him and then after a while he'd drive you so crazy, you'd pay him to go away, you know, give him a divorce? Then me and him was gonna…opp…hang on, I think the shower just went off…. Yeah, it did. Okay, gotta go, hon… oh, one more thing, that book dealie? Part of the con, sweetheart. You ever see a manuscript? Didn't think so. When you see lover boy tonight, tell him Spanky said goodbye, okay? Opp, here he comes. Ciao."*

The silence that followed in the courtroom was painful. You could've heard a fly fart. Even Judge Delridge seemed stunned. Uneasy moments passed before Wally stood up and broke the reverie.

"Your Honor, at this time the defense would like to request a stay in these proceedings to discuss a motion to amend the indictment."

Delridge looked at Tolby, who in turn shrugged his acquiescence. He didn't care, he had this verdict in the bag.

"Very well Mr. Clifford," Delridge said. "The witness may step down. However, Mrs. Erskine, assuming your counsel will want to cross-examine, I must remind you that you are still under oath and may be recalled at any time. Meanwhile, court is adjourned and the jury is dismissed until nine a.m. tomorrow. Counselors? I will see both of you in my chambers, now."

As Sara stepped down from the witness chair, Wally met her in front of the bench, conferred briefly with her before heading off to the judge's chambers. Sara's face clouded up and tears started rolling again as she watched her uncle walk away.

In judges' chamber, after Wally explained his amendment to the indictment, Eldridge asked, "So, Mr. Clifford, by requesting to change the indictment, you're admitting that the death of Carl Erskine was not an accident, and that your client has lied under oath, is that correct?"

"Yes, sir."

Tolby laughed and said, "Really, your Honor? What the defense is asking for here is unprecedented and is an obvious attempt to delay proceedings so they can look for grounds for a mistrial."

"On the contrary, Mr. Tolby," Wally said. "Citing a case similar to this one, People versus Connors, 420 CT, in 2012 in the State of Pennsylvania the defense was allowed to amend the indictment at the eleventh hour of the trial, and given that ninety-nine percent of all evidence and testimony up to that point was qualified and uncontested, and because the defendant rectified her testimony, the charge of perjury was withdrawn and the trial continued without missing one day. In fact, your honor, if you will allow, tomorrow morning I will be brief with my cross-examination of Sar, ah…Mrs. Erskine, and will forego my closing argument so you may hand this case directly to the jury."

Judge Delridge took a breath and said, "I'm aware of the case you mentioned counselor, but I'll need to peruse it before I make my decision."

"Your Honor! That's exactly the tactic---"

Eldridge raised his hand to stop Tolby. "And, I will give you my decision at nine o'clock tomorrow morning in court. Either way I rule, this trial will continue as scheduled.

The next morning at nine o'clock, Judge Eldridge informed the jury of the amendment to the indictment and instructions on how to proceed. Wally, as promised, immediately began his cross-examination of Sara.

"Mrs. Erskine, going back to the night your husband was killed, what did you do after you listened to the voicemail message?"

"I…I went into the study."

"To look for the manuscript?"

"Yes. I had told Charlie once that he should keep a printed version to back up his work, just in case something happened to his laptop. He said that that was a good idea and I noticed a few times when he was on his computer, he would print a few pages and then put them in one of the drawers in the desk that he kept locked."

"Locked? Why? Was he afraid someone might steal it, or that you might look at it?"

"I don't know. Both, maybe."

"Did you find the manuscript, Mrs. Erskine?"

"Yes. The key was in the main drawer."

"What else was in the drawer?"

"A pistol. I thought maybe that's why he kept the drawer locked."

"Approximately what time was this?"

"It was just before Charlie got home. About eight, I guess."

"Did you read any of the manuscript?"

"Just the title."

"And what was the title on the manuscript Mrs. Erskine?"

"It was called, 'The Big Shuffle', by Charles Erskine."

"Did you read any further?"

Sara took a moment, gathered herself, and answered; "All the other pages were blank."

"Mrs. Erskine, were you at the desk looking at the manuscript when your husband came home and entered the study?"

"Yes."

"Please tell the court what happened then."

"Charlie saw what I was looking at and got mad. He kinda rushed toward me and said *whadya think you're doing!?* Then he called me a dumb, uh, you know… he used the C word."

"The C word, Mrs. Erskine?"

"Yes, you know, c-u-n-t."

148

"What did you do then, Mrs. Erskine?"

"I shot him."

Wally looked at the jury, then to the judge; "Nothing further, your Honor. The defense rests."

The jury deliberated for 43 minutes before they came back with a verdict. They would've been back sooner but two of the jurors had to use the restroom first. One of the female jurors said later that it was the toilet seat thing for her. One of the men mentioned the driving in the left lane bothered him. In any event, all of the jurors agreed with Wally's new defense strategy; Charlie Erskine's death was indeed a justifiable homicide.

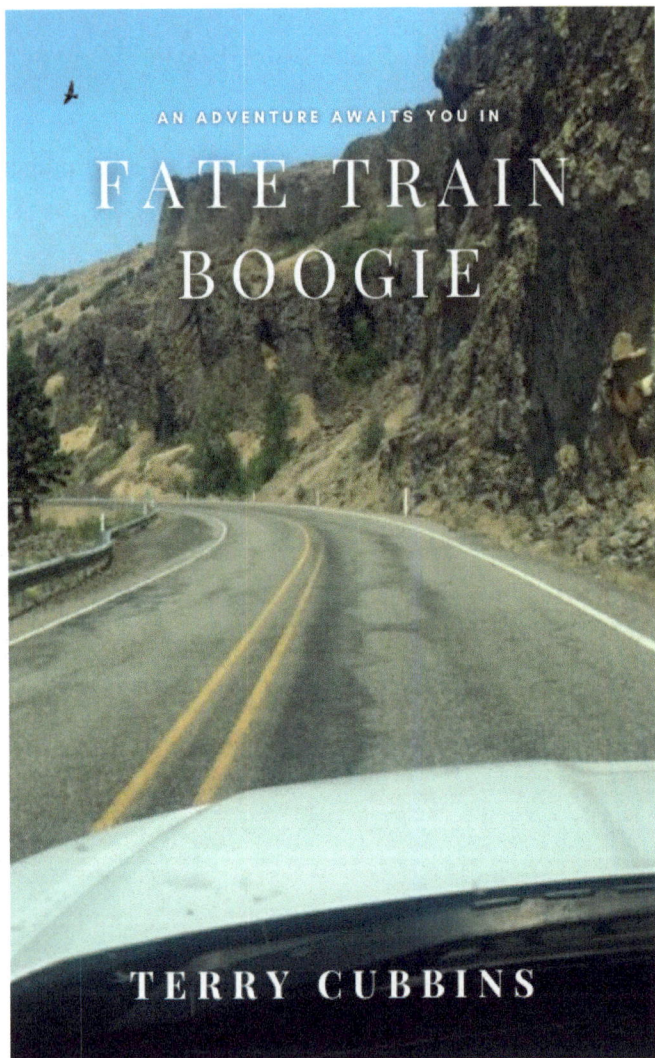

AN ADVENTURE AWAITS YOU IN

FATE TRAIN BOOGIE

TERRY CUBBINS

FATE TRAIN BOOGIE

The rock had been sitting on the canyon rim high above the valley pretty much since time began. A rock of ages you might say. Four billion years ago, give or take, the rock had been part of a massive cliff that had formed when the earth farted its innards outwards. Sometime during the rocks' adolescents, probably following an ice age, the rock calved and became the shape that it was now. Grand in size, possibly weighing more than five tons. In all of its millions of trips around the sun, the rock had remained relatively in place in what is now known as the Cascade Mountain Range in Central Washington State.

Now, in August of the year 2019 AD, the rock was getting ready to roll. A breeze had picked up and minor temblors jiggled the terrain. Tiny bits of gravel around the base of the rock were trickling away, down towards Highway 970 and the Yakima River below.

Meanwhile, forty-three-year-old Calvin Dupree and his nine-month-old yellow lab, Marvel, were traveling on Highway 970 and had just passed milepost 93 driving west toward Seattle in Cal's 89' Ford pickup truck.

It was a nice afternoon for a drive with temperatures in the mid 70's. Cal, who worked as an electronics engineer at a nearby radio station, had the cruise control on, the radio up and the windows rolled down. Marvel rode shotgun with his nose resting on the windowsill, nostrils twitching. Man and beast were feeling pretty good, as well they should, for it's not every day you stumble on a cure for cancer. While they cruised, Willie Nelson came on the radio,

'On the Road Again…'

But things hadn't always been so rosy. It was just a year ago that Cal's wife decided to hit the road herself, leaving Cal alone in a two-bedroom rambler near the edge of town. For the first three months Cal moaned around the house telling himself that he needed to get on with his life. He needed to *get* a life!

Then one day as he was looking out the window at his front lawn and white picket fence, it hit him; *I can get a dog now!*

Cal began his search for a new pal at the local animal shelter. When he spotted Marvel, he stuck his finger through the wire gage to get the dog's attention. Two seconds later, it was love at first bite. The first thing Cal did when he got Marvel home was to go through the house trying to puppy-proof it. He moved all the chewable things including electrical cords and drapes. He put newspapers down. He did everything he could think of inside the house. But as Cal soon learned, that the challenge wasn't inside the house, it was outside. Marvel was marvelous at digging under the fence and mindlessly sniffing and chasing whatever lay beyond.

After training attempts failed to keep Marvel from wandering, Cal had an 'Invisible Fence' buried around the perimeter of his house. Initially, Cal didn't like the idea of his dog being shocked through a battery-operated collar, but when he was told that it was more radio waves than electricity, he felt better about it. Marvel got 'bit' just once during a training session with his new collar in place and then never ventured past the buried line again. Marvel didn't seem to hold any of this confinement against Cal, after all, most of the time before Cal left the house, he swapped out the zapper collar with a regular one and took him with him. Even to the radio station where all the employees high-foured him and gave him a treat.

Cal had always been interested in science and electronics, but that didn't keep him from driving a pickup truck, listening to country music and having a beer now and then. It was back when Cal was getting over his divorce that he got the bad news from his veterinarian. Cal had taken Marvel in for a check-up because he seemed to be losing weight and lacking energy. The diagnose was a cancerous brain tumor.

"It's in an area that we can't radiate or operate on Cal. I'm sorry," said Doctor Val, "you have a few months, maybe."

Two weeks later, Cal fertilized his lawn with some left-over material he had in his storage shed behind the house. When he picked up the sack of fertilizer it ripped apart and some of the granules spilled out on the ground. Cal noticed that the fertilizer was old and had formed clumps. It had also changed color from its original whiteish-yellow to a pale brown. After spreading the fertilizer, Cal returned to the storage shed and stopped in his tracks; Marvel was licking up what was left of the fertilizer that had spilled earlier. Cal immediately called his veterinarian, Doctor Val. "Better bring him in," she told him.

Cal grabbed Marvel in his arms and jogged toward the street where his pickup was parked. As they crossed the invisible fence line, Marvel let out a yelp. Cal cursed himself for forgetting to take Marvel's electronic collar off before crossing the line but he didn't have time to dwell on it. Ten minutes later, at the vets, Marvel was immediately taken into the examination room while Cal waited in the reception area. As he waited, he couldn't help but wonder if this was the end for his new pal. Forty-five minutes later,

Doctor Val came out and told Cal, "Right now he seems to be alright but I'd like to run some more tests and keep him overnight for observation."

The next day, Cal was at the vets first thing in the morning. Doctor Val greeted him with the news. "Marvel seems to be doing very well. He's alert, eaten food, and shows no ill effects from ingesting the fertilizer."

Cal was greatly relieved but noticed a puzzled look on the vet's face. "Is there something else doc? The tumor?"

"As a matter of fact, there is Cal." Doctor Val said. "I'm not sure what to make of this yet, but I took x-rays while Marvel was under a sedative...."

Cal took a breath.

"...and it appears the tumor has *shrunk* a little. Even the blood tests came in somewhat favorable from what they were before."

"What? Really? How could...?"

Doctor Val shrugged. "I don't know for sure," she said. "I took a few other x-rays just to see if the equipment was in good working order. Everything checked out. Right now, all I can say is …take Marvel home. Keep an eye on him. We'll see you again in two weeks and take more pictures."

Cal happily took Marvel home, astonished by how much energy his dog had. Over the next few weeks, they took up their regular schedule of going everywhere together. A nearby lake for some swimming and fetching. Frisbee in the back yard. Naps together on the back porch. Cal cherished every moment knowing that the next visit to the vets might have different results. Cal tried to remain optimistic but guardedly so. When it came time to take Marvel back to the vets, Cal remembered to take the battery collar off this time. Cal sat in the waiting area again, looking at all the dog and cat diet pamphlets and notices of lost and founds pets that he had looked at before. Finally, Doctor Val came in to the lobby…smiling.

"Everything looks good, another clean showing. Marvel's sedated right now but if you want to come back in a couple of hours you can take him home. Just don't look him in the mouth."

"Wha…?"

"You know, gift horse and all."

As the days passed and Marvel showed no signs of slowing down, Cal became obsessed with the recovery. *What had happened to the tumor? How did the blood cell count change?* Cal began researching everything he could about cancer treatment in dogs as well as humans. His research took him to a man named John Kanzius, a retired TV engineer and ham radio operator whose design of radio transmitter that could treat cancerous tumors had gained him national attention in 2008. *60 Minutes* had a feature on him and his theory. Kanzius, who was diagnosed with leukemia in 2002, had created a radio frequency generating machine in his garage that he used to heat solutions of copper sulfate. He then injected the sulfate in a hotdog to pose as a tumor. When he induced radio waves through the hotdogs, he found that only the copper sulfate grew warm whereas the rest of the area stayed cold. Cal then looked up the ingredients in fertilizer. *Sulfate.* Bingo! He also learned that John Kanzius died in 2008, but his copper sulfate theory was still being looked at. Cal theoretically connected the dots and then added one of his own. The procedure was simple. He was ready to advance his theory but first he needed someone to listen to him. Now, at 4:33 Cal and Marvel were passing milepost 89 as Willie was crooning…

'I just can't wait to get on the road again…'

Meanwhile, a half a mile to the south, sixty-year-old, Tugg McWubbins was on his back porch, soaking in his Jacuzzi, a chilled beer glass full of St Pauli's Girl at hand. His radio tuned to the same station that Cal was listening to. McWubbins, somewhat of an aging hipster, had ingested a marijuana brownie earlier and was now in the process of contemplating his navel. As Willie wailed, McWubbins' attention was diverted to a tiny flying insect that had fallen into the water. As the bug struggled, McWubbins thought about the significance, or lack thereof, of the situation. *If there are eight- billion humans on Earth, there's gotta be at least twenty-*

katrillion insects. What's the difference if this particular bug lives or dies? The thought made McWubbins think about his own mortality as well. *Why am I even here? I've not gone forth and multiplied. I have no family. A few friends, sure, but I mean nothing. I'm not a doctor or a teacher or even a good welder. I can't sing. I'm not an artist, although I did paint the backside of the garage recently.*

In the end, McWubbins rationalized that maybe saving one of God's creatures might just put him over the top in case there was ever a question on judgment day. He reached for the screen he used for cleaning the Jacuzzi and in one motion, lifted the bug out of the water and tapped it free on the porch hand railing next to the tub. The bug stumbled around like a drunken sailor, struggling to unfold its wet wings, but it was alive. Satisfied that he had done the right thing, McWubbins settled back down into the tub. With his attention now back on his navel, he hadn't noticed the small sparrow-like bird on the far end of the railing who was watching his bug-saving rescue with interest. The bird hopped closer, stopped and twisted its little head around a couple of times, checking for danger, finding none, he swooped in, grabbed the bug off of McWubbins' porch railing and flew north toward Hiway 970.

'The life I love, is making music with my friends…'

Cal was approaching a curve and milepost 88, when suddenly the bird from McWubbins' porch flew in front of his windshield. *Holy shi..*! Cal hit the brakes. A heartbeat later the rock of ages filled the windshield. Cal ducked and threw his arms in front of him as the behemoth blasted by them, missing them by inches. The rock flew down the slope, bouncing crazily before finally crashing in the middle of the river. Birds exploded upwards, shrieking away. Trees near the river danced and swayed. Water rolled in a direction that it wasn't used to. Cal's truck seemed to wobble on its own over to the side of the road before it stopped. Small rocks tinked off of the truck as dust settled around them. Cal lowered his arms, peeked at Marvel, then slowly pushed himself up and looked at the carnage below.

"My God, Marv, that was close! If that bird

hadn't of flown in front of us, that rock woulda crushed us!" He stared at the scene below for a few moments before looking back at his pal. "And who woulda got the word out, huh?"

Meanwhile, McWubbins was out of the tub, toweling off and Willie was wrapping up…

'And I can't wait to get on the road again…'

As he started to pull the cover over the Jacuzzi, McWubbins saw another bug crash-land in the water. He watched it struggle and swirl around for awhile, then he shrugged and pulled the cover closed, "Sorry, pal. Can't save everyone, you know."

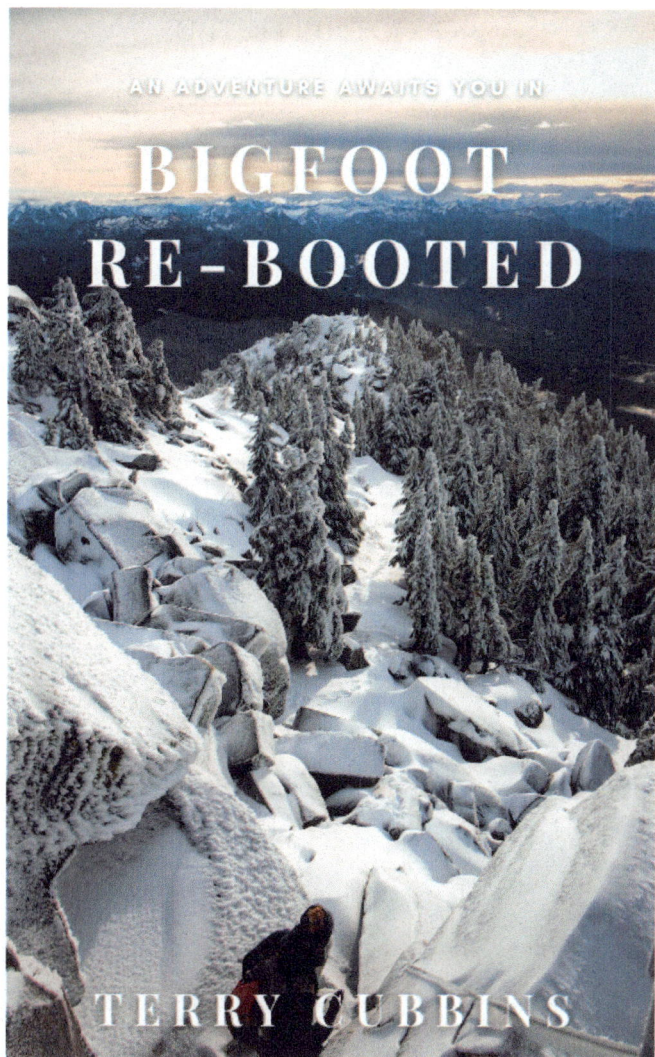

AN ADVENTURE AWAITS YOU IN

BIGFOOT RE-BOOTED

TERRY CUBBINS

BIGFOOT REBOOTED

"You say Carl, called?"

"Yep."

"He ask for money again?"

"Nope."

"Really? What's he want then?

Danny was sitting on the couch sipping local pale ale and thumbing through a photo magazine. Cindy was in the kitchen preparing their Friday night chicken stir-fry, a glass of white wine on the counter. This was all taking place in their condo on the Icicle River near the town of Leavenworth, Washington.

"He's hoping to get a booth in the show with you guys," Cindy said, continuing their conversation.

"What? He's a photographer now? I thought he was a writer?"

"Well, yes he is a writer. He's in town to promote his latest book."

"Ah…wait," Danny said, smiling. "You're telling me that Carl wants to promote a book with a lot of words in it and everything, at a photo exhibit. An exhibit that displays, ah, how shall I put this...photos? And just how long were you married to this man?"

Cindy stopped chopping chicken, picked up her wine, took a healthy sip and with knife in hand, eye-balled daggers at Danny. Danny could read the degrees in the daggers and judged them to be temperate. Cindy had a bit of a buzz going but it looked good on her.

Cindy Collins was a University of Washington grad, 32 years old and somewhat of a small package at 5'2, 118 lbs. But her athletic figure and ginger-colored hair should have been a clue that there was more to the lady than a small mass issue. Her green eyes seemed to flicker when she smiled which was often. She was smart and well respected as the Director of the Chamber of Commerce in Leavenworth.

The weekend she came to town to interview for the director's job is when she met Danny. She had planned an extra day for a little fun and reserved a spot on a white water raft trip on the Wenatchee River. Turned out, Danny was the guide that day and after only two wet hours on the river, they had exchanged phone numbers. That day on the river also happened to be the day that Cindy's divorce became official from Carl Sndyer; a six foot, blond, blue-eyed, car salesman, actor, Hollywood stuntman, inventor, monk, model, writer and photographer.

Danny Larson on the other hand, had never been married, was 31, 5'11' 175 lbs. Besides guiding white water rafts and fishing trips, he was a professional wild life and naturalist photographer. He was born and raised in the area and had a degree in Psychology from Central Washington University. He would be considered a catch by most young ladies; shoulder length brown hair, dark brown eyes and a two inch scar near his left eye to add to the interest. The scar was courtesy of a drunken fly caster one day when Danny's attention had wandered.

"Okay, okay. I know Carl's got a big heart…but a tiny brain." Danny knew he was pushing it with the tiny brain part so he hurried on with his next question before taking a swallow of beer. "So, what's his book about?"

"Bigfoot," Cindy said.

Danny suddenly coughed and gurgled while beer sprizled out of his nose. He bent over and continued to cough while Cindy hurried over with a dish towel in her hands, concerned. She stayed concerned until she saw Danny trying to smile between coughs. When he croaked, "Bigfoot? Really?" she slapped the towel at him and went back to the kitchen. When she was within reach of her wine, she asked, "And what's wrong with Bigfoot?"

Danny had a red bandana out, trying to wipe the smile and everything else off his face. When he found his voice again, he said, "Aw, Bigfoot was okay in his time, I guess. But vampires and zombies pretty much did him in. He's passé now."

"Oh, so, you're an expert on Bigfoot now, huh?"

"As a matter o fact, I is, "Danny said, feeling his

own beer buzz. "You see, vampires, zombies and even werewolves work because they can morph in and out of reality, they don't have to be real, you know? But Bigfoot is solid stuff. He can't just wisp away, he's gotta leave tracks and turds and hairs and shit."

"You just said, turds *and* shit."

"Well, you know, he's gotta be more than just one old fuzzy picture strolling through the woods that we've all seen countless times. Kinda like the Loch Nest Monster photo, the humps in the lake? I think the technology these days, satellites, radar, sonar, heat sensors, you know, stuff like Google Earth have pretty much put those stories to rest. There's camera's everywhere. If you're livin' and breathin', you've got we call a signature, you'll show up somewhere, sometime, on something. You can't escape no mo, you know?"

"Who's we?"

"Huh?"

"You said, you've got what we call a signature. Who's we?"

Danny felt that they were getting away from the subject about Carl bringing a book to a photo expo but decided that the best tact to take at that point was to mention how good things smelled in the kitchen. Cindy was quick to agree, "You're right, let's eat."

All was well through dinner with no further mention of Carl or the upcoming exhibit, although later that night in bed, when everyone but the Sandman had cometh, it was a different story. Danny was stifling a yawn and basking in après sex when a thought crossed his mind; "Hey, wait a minute, wasn't the show sold out?"

Cindy was half asleep, nestled with her back to him. "Ahh... what?"

"The show? Isn't it always sold out? Like a month or more in advance?"

"Mmm…yeah, usually… we had a late cancellation."

"So, Carl gets his book in there?"

"Hmm... Maybe."

"His book has photos?

"I guess."

"Of what?"

"Mountains, forests...you know..."

"But none of ol'Bigdick?"

Cindy lifted her head, "Look, why don't you ask him yourself? He's coming to the chamber at noon on Monday to show us what he has, okay?" Then she looked away and flipped her pillow. Danny had crossed the line and he knew it. The following silence was telling. He leaned over, kissed Cindy on the back of her neck and said, "Okay, 'nite."

Cindy flipped her pillow again, punched it and said, 'Yep,' into it.

Cindy had always been honest with Danny and why he needn't be jealous of Carl. She said she had never seen Carl as a sexy stud but more like a lovable puppy, at first, anyway. But when the puppy didn't grow out of his grace period and continued to mess and chew, then that became a problem. Fortunately, Cindy and Carl were both mature enough to realize early on that they'd rushed things and that they'd made a mistake. They agreed that they'd both probably be happier if they could go their own way. Their divorce was amicable, they agreed to stay in touch and they parted friends. About the only thing that rankled Danny was every time one of Carl's business ventures failed, he would call on Cindy to fulfill his duty as the toucher.

Before meeting Cindy, Danny lived in a small cabin that his Grandfather had left him just off the Icicle River and about five miles upstream from Leavenworth. When Cindy got the job in town and bought the condo, Danny later moved in with her and shared the mortgage, however he kept the cabin for the times when either one of them might feel he needed to go to his room.

Saturday morning, when Danny and Cindy got up, there were three inches of fresh snow on their deck. Cindy fixed breakfast but seemed a little quiet. Danny decided that after shoveling the deck, he'd do some winterizing around the condo then go up to the cabin and finish winterizing it too… probably take the rest of the weekend up there.

When Danny was at the door, getting ready to leave, he yelled out, "I'm goin'". He didn't hear anything for a moment or two and was about to leave when Cindy came to the door. She kissed him and patted his chest. "Don't forget to come by the Chamber at noon if you wanna see what Carl's book is about, okay? Otherwise I was hoping we could meet for lunch at Sturzt's, around one, one-fifteen?"

By twelve-thirty Monday afternoon, there were two more inches of snow on the ground when Danny pulled into the Chambers' parking lot in town. As he walked through the entry door an old time door bell jingled overhead, announcing his presence to Cindy and about twelve other people huddled around a table at the far end of the only room. Cindy smiled at him but the others just gave him a cursory glance then went back to looking at photographs and charts that Carl was intently showing them. As Danny drew up to the gathering, Carl looked up, smiled and said, "Hey,

172

man, how you doin'?'"

Before Danny could react, someone said, "Carl, why don't you show him the picture you just showed us? See if he can find Bigfoot."

"Yeah," someone else said. "Show him."

Carl looked around, shrugged and then pulled a large color photo from some other pictures and placed it on the table. It was a photograph of a forested mountainside with a small creek running through the bottom of the picture. Danny was immediately impressed, the framing, the lighting, the composition, it was all there. He kept studying the photo forgetting he was supposed to find Waldo somewhere in it.

"Better show him, Carl, he'll never find him," said one of the onlookers.

"Look at the bottom left, where the creek pools against a log. He's in the background," said another.

Carl watched Danny's eyes go to the bottom left of the photo and began searching, but when they didn't appear to come up with anything, Carl pointed to a spot between tree limbs and brush near the creek and suddenly the likeness of Bigfoots' face, neck and shoulders jumped into focus for Danny. Danny looked at it for a moment, said, "Nice shot", turned to Cindy, "See you at Sturzts'," then walked away.

Forty-five minutes later, Cindy caught up with Danny at Sturzt's restaurant. He was sitting in a booth with two menus, a cup of coffee and a white wine. She slid in opposite him, took a sip of wine and said; "Nice shot?"

"What?"

"You never see or talk to Carl and then when you do, it's two words; 'nice shot?' You might have well have just said, 'fuck you' to him. There wasn't a lot of heat in Cindy's statement and she had a mischievous look on her face when she said it, so Danny's reply was made in kind.

"Yeah and I could've said, 'photo-shopped' to him…or is photo-shopped one word?"

Cindy nodded, "Okay, but what about me? Me, whom you haven't seen or felt for two days; 'see you at lunch? What's with you, big-time?"

"I'm sorry about that, Cin, it's just when I saw

that face in the trees, I...I kinda lost it."

Cindy shook her head. "I know, I know, but if you were there earlier you could have seen some other stuff Carl had that was actually pretty interesting; pictures of tracks in the snow and caves and theories about underground networks and how a Bigfoot family survives, even theories about how climate change might force humans to start to living underground like Bigfoot to escape the heat at some point."

"Shut up."

"Why, may I ask?"

"You sound like a commercial, like you're pitchin' him."

"Carl or Bigfoot?"

"Either. Both."

When Cindy looked away without saying anything, Danny slowly started nodding his head. He was nodding when the waiter arrived; he resumed nodding after the waiter left with their lunch order.

"So," Danny said, "Carl's gonna be in the show, right?"

"C'mon, honey, the show's this Friday. We need to fill the booth."

"I know, but what about a little integrity here? We've got a history to protect you know. For years--"

"I know you're talking about the exhibit now," Cindy Interrupted, "but I know what's behind those black and white pictures on the walls at the Chamber too. The fur trading outpost stuff, the mining, the sawmill and railroad. I also know that when those industries left the area, this town was pretty much stuck in neutral and just struggled along to keep the lights on...until it went Bavarian and tourism saved the day."

Danny shrugged, "Sweetie, I'm sure the Bavarian Alps are beautiful, but I sometimes wonder why this town didn't promote its own history and what it had to offer first, then maybe there'd be a place in Germany trying to look like us."

Cindy smiled, "You know, I think we can use you at the Chamber. Whaddya say?"

Danny was cornered. Almost a third of his annual income came from the three days of the show, not just from photos sold or future film work but from down-payments on reservations for guiding and river rafting later in the year. The Leavenworth Outdoor Photo Expo was never advertized for more than a photo exhibit but it was common knowledge that every photographer in the show had a side hustle of some sort.

Danny threw up his hands and surrendered, "Okay, okay, Jesus! Whip me, beat me, hit me with your best shot. Might as well let Bigfoot stomp on me too."

"Ah, c'mon," Cindy said. "It'll be fine. By this time next week Carl will be long gone and everything will be back to normal." Then she reached for his hand, "And we can talk about that whipping part later tonight."

Lunch arrived and conversation flowed comfortably. After desert, Cindy slid out of the booth and joined Danny on his side. She brought her coffee with her and snuggled up to him. "Brr, its cold." Neither said anything until Cindy said, "By the way, you know that Carl is traveling in his van, don't you?"

"Yeah, you told me."

"Well, I guess the heater in it broke down."

"Oh?"

"Pretty cold out there."

"So? He get a motel?"

"No, he said he had to spend most of his money to get into the show."

"Oh, poor baby. I guess he'll just have to put another blanket on."

"It's not usually this cold, though, is it?"

"Goddamn it, Cindy, you just can't keep bailing him out. You wanna get him a room, don't you?"

"Well...I was wondering...how would you feel about... a cabin?"

Later that afternoon, much to his disbelief, Danny found himself showing Carl around the cabin. Carl noticed a topographical map unfolded on the kitchen table and stopped to look at it.

"This looks like an interesting area," Carl said as he tapped his finger on the map. "A-24, huh? Tough terrain, elevation changes, rocks, cliffs and stuff. It could be excellent habitat for certain creatures."

178

"Yeah, well, that's up by where I got a Canada Lynx two years ago," Danny said, "In fact I'm—"

"I know you're a skeptic, Danny, you mind if I show you something?" Before Danny could say no, Carl pulled some sketches and photos out of his backpack. They were drawings of an underground tunnel and cave system that would make a 1950's bunker salesman's proud. Carl launched into his theory on how Bigfoot probably lived in a system like this. Carl also had a couple of long distance shots of what looked like smaller versions of Bigfoot. "This could be an offspring," Carl said. He showed Danny photos of Bigfoot tracks that were taken years ago and compared them to photos that Carl said he had recently taken. They were smaller. It was hard denying Carl's enthusiasm but ten minutes later, Danny excused himself, got in his truck and left, saying he had to get home.

Danny made it about three miles down the road before he pulled over. Was he feeling sorry for Carl? Maybe he could look at his heater? Maybe the dumb shit hasn't got the right valve on or something? Danny turned around and drove back to the cabin. As he was pulling into the drive he saw Carl coming out of the side door of his van pulling a green duffel bag with him. When Carl looked up and saw Danny, he pushed the bag back into the van and slid the door shut. He hurried up to Danny's truck.

"Forget something?"

"I thought maybe I could look at your heater, I'm pretty---"

"Oh, no, that's alright. But thanks, I'll get'er fixed next week, no problem."

"I don't mind. Does the pilot light come on?"

"Yeah, well, look, Danny, really, you don't have to mess with it now, okay?"

Danny noticed Carl's voice had taken a certain edge to it. It didn't take Danny long to get his truck turned around and get gone again.

Two years previous, Danny had won top honors with a stunning photo of an endangered Canada Lynx staring out of a snow cave. He had actually set out that day looking for the elu. ve

180

wolverine, the pound for pound bad-ass of the woods, but still had yet to see one. He was planning on going hunting for one again after the show before the snow got any deeper.

When the weekend came and the show opened at the high school gym, there was no more avoiding Carl. Turned out there was more interest in ol'Bigdick than Danny thought. It was like someone laid out a speed bump in front of Carl's booth; a back up of foot traffic there all day with folks buying his book and bombarding him with questions.

"What's the difference between Bigfoot and Sasquatch?"

"None, they're the same," he would say.

"So, there's more than one Bigfoot?"

"Yes, we think so."

"Are Bigfoots mean?"

"Not unless provoked."

That night, being Friday, it was Danny's turn to cook the stir fry and Cindy's turn to watch, she did so from a corner stool at the kitchen island.

"You sure Carl didn't affect any of your

181

business?" she asked.

Danny stopped what he was doing and looked at Cindy. "No. Why'd you ask me that again?"

Cindy put her glass of wine down, went over to Danny, patted his butt, then said," Oh, I don't know, you seem a little quiet, and I thought I detected a little extra 'ommph' a minute ago when you sliced the chicken." She opened the fridge, got Danny a fresh beer and went back to her seat. Danny took a minute, smirked and said, "You think I was hard on that chicken? Wait'll you see what I do with this onion." He took a swig of beer. "Well, okay, yeah, Carl was a distraction, but not just for me, for everyone, so you should be concerned too, but his act will wither away soon. By the way, what're Carl's plans after he leaves town?"

"Keep writing and researching, I guess. He's on a roll now, you know?"

"Keep writing and making up stuff you mean?"

"Oh, Danny, just let him go. Let him have his fun. His photos are good, right? And, he has stirred up some new theories, you know, like with those underground systems?, And Bigfoot's new diets and smaller Bigfoots? God... did I just say that?"

"You did, and don't ever say it again in my lifetime."

Overall, the show was deemed a success and Danny did almost as much business as he had the previous year. Carl had his heater fixed and was out of the cabin by Tuesday. For Danny, it was time to let bygones be bygones and move on...again.

He began prepping for his three day, two night photo Safari. His primary target would be a wolverine again but, like the terrain around Leavenworth, the mountain peaks alone were worth the trip. The moon would be entering a new phase which could offer possibilities of some black and whites in concert with those peaks, but those shots would depend on the weather of course and Danny would be prepared. It would mean camping alone and probably out of cell phone service for a day or two but that was nothing new for him either, it was a time he was looking forward to, turning off all media and renewing his survival skills. His checklist for his trip included letting Cindy check his checklist. When she was through she would say, "Be careful, okay?"

"I will."

"Don't do anything stupid."

"I won't."

"I love you."

"I love you, too.

Then she would say, "I wish you had a dog to go with you."

It was snowing lightly the morning Danny left. On the way to the old caved-in cabin that he used for a camp he was encouraged by an abundance of game tracks he saw. He got a couple of good shots of two bald eagles that were perched totem-pole fashion atop an old fir snag and he spent some time trying to capture the wrath of a piss-off red-tailed mama hawk who was flying sorties against him defending her nest. Eventually he made it to the cabin and set up shop. He let Cindy know he'd arrived then took a couple of shots in and around the old cabin in what was left of the snowy afternoon light. After a dinner of dried tortellini and red wine from his boda bag he signed off with Cindy and settled into his sleeping bag accompanied by the sound of an owl in the distance and some pack rats scratching around close by.

The next morning, daylight was filtering through falling snow as Danny eased over the ridge of the ravine where he'd seen his lynx two years earlier. He settled in a group of boulders above the ridgeline and began his watch. His field of vision was about 270 degrees and he could see about two hundred yards in each direction. He wasn't there more than twenty minutes before he saw movement in the trees and brush below him and to his right. The combination of snow and daylight breaking through make it difficult to tell what he was seeing, the zoom lenses just blurred things more. At first Danny thought it was a bear with insomnia or something. Whatever it was it was moving slightly away from him and downward.

Danny watched as it made its way through some brush. It paused for a moment, and then stepped into a clearing. Danny's heart jumped. The animal stood six foot tall, had hairy arms and legs, greenish brown fur, and yeah, two big feet.

Jesus, Christ! It looks real! Danny instinctively began snapping shots with one ear waiting to hear Carl yell, "Cut!" The creature ambled down to the bottom of the ravine, then stopped and looked back up the side of the slope. Its movements seemed like an animated cartoon character, twisting and raising its head, looking around in different directions. Then it walked back down and continued on its journey. When it looked like it was going to climb over a rise to the north, Danny quickly got ready to follow. When the animal, or whatever it was, disappeared over the rise, Danny gave it a ten count before moving. When it didn't reappear, and film crews didn't materialize out of the trees, Danny hustled after the creature.

When he came over the rise at he saw the animal prancing around an old fir tree. Danny had closed the distance between the two to probably seventy-five yards but kept enough foliage between them to stay hidden. The snow had begun to fall at a much heavier rate and Danny switched lenses and tried to steady his hand and heartbeat.

Soon the thing stopped its gyrations and returned to the trail. Danny was mesmerized by the actions and fluidity of the thing and worked hard to keep it in focus as the thing now drew nearer, getting larger, its face filling the view finder...Oh, shit, wait!

Danny looked quickly behind him and thought about his options; should he stay where he was and keep shooting? Try to move to another location without being seen? Or stand up and yell and see what happens?

He went with option of scrambling back and slightly upward towards some shrubs in front of some rocky outcroppings, almost in the same direction from where he had just come from. When he scrunched down and looked back, he saw the thing had just cleared the rise and was walking with its head down almost like it was tired. Danny gained his breath

187

and started shooting again, but as he did, the thing stopped, looked in Danny's direction and started climbing the small grade toward him.

What the hell? It couldn't be tracking him could it? Their tracks were still at least fifty feet apart. *Had it seen him? Was it smelling him?*

Crouching now, Danny retreated again, up to a rock cliff and into a small crevice. When he got there he turned and looked back. The animal was coming up the hill toward him and started going through some gyrations again. This time, Danny took his gun out first and set it next to him before picking up his camera.

Again Danny was fascinated as he filmed the animal and the thought crossed his mind; he was now clearly referring to it as an animal. He thought about Cindy and how she felt about animals. What would Cindy think of this situation? *Jesus Christ! Start yelling! With camera in hand or with gun in hand?* Seconds before Danny had to make that decision, the animal took a couple of steps to its left and sat down heavily behind a boulder in small cove. Danny was slightly above him, only twenty feet away. He had stopped filming for some reason and just watched as the animal sat slumped with its head down. *Is it hurt? Is it lost? Or just tired?* Slowly it raised its head and put its elbows and wrists together as if tied together; then in one swift motion, yanked hard and all the fur on both arms and hands seemed to fall off right off, exposing two normal looking human arms and hands. *WTF!*

Next, it reached along its neck and began pulling up flaps and releasing fasteners of some sort and soon the head came rolling off… and up popped another one; it was Carl! *Goddamn son-of-a bitch! I knew it. I fuckin' knew it. Goddamn him! Goddamn you! You dirty, son-of-a bitch…*

It took all of Danny's self control not to jump down and beat the livin' shit out of Carl right then and there but he knew he had to get this on film. He hoped to hell that Carl wouldn't hear his camera or the pounding of his heart as he started shooting again. *Jesus, God. You dirty mother…*

189

Carl continued to peel apart the suit that he'd been wearing until he was stripped down to his long underwear. Then he got up and took a couple of steps, reached behind a rock and pulled out his green duffle bag. He removed a camo parka, boots and gloves from the bag and then carefully folded the Bigfoot suit back into it. At this point, Danny was shaking so hard he was afraid he was going to drop his camera.

After dressing, Carl walked over and pulled down a game camera from above the entrance to the cove. He made some adjustments, looked at it, then said out loud; "Time delay? No! No! I wanted Motion! Not fuckin' time delay! Aw, shit! He shoved the duffle bag behind a rock, arranged some brush over it and then after sticking his head outside the cove and looking carefully around, he started back down the way he'd come. And Danny had it all on film.

Hey Carl, where you goin', man? I've got something right here on my camera you can look at, you piece of shit. Then he realized that Carl probably

190

had another game cam set up by tree just over the knoll and was probably on his way to check it out.

Danny was pissed. Really pissed. But, not enough to stay where he was and really shoot Carl when and if he came back. Well, maybe he could. If Carl came back and put the suit on again, then Danny could shoot him and claim the thing tried to attack him. Self-defense. Or, maybe not shoot him dead, just wing him in his ass, or put one in his upper lip or something.

The absurdity of those options meant that Danny's intrinsic anger relief- value was doing its job. The expanding emotional energy was segueing to the clear thinking department of his brain; if he wasn't going to beat on Carl's head, he might as well fuck with it.

Danny wanted the duffle bag for further evidence but he already had enough to carry back to camp as it was and with the snow coming down harder all the time, he didn't want to get bogged down in case a piss-ant like Carl could track him. As soon as

Carl was out of sight, Danny dropped down, grabbed the duffle bag and went over to other side of the grotto and stuck it in a one of the holes of the honeycombed rock and covered it up. Before leaving, he replaced the brush and stones where Carl had originally hid the bag and then he climbed out of the cavern and made his way back to camp.

At the camp, Danny immediately looked at the pictures he taken of Carl. He was disappointed in the clarity of some of them but the proof was there; Carl's goose was cooked. Next he sent Cindy a text, it was more of a test than anything, he doubted that he'd have a connection with all the snow but he thumbed:

Have stunning shots. Snowing hard now, but all good. May come home early.

Surprisingly, Cindy answered:

Great! Can't wait to see photos. Stay safe.

It was really hard for Danny not to announce the news about Carl but he knew it would be better to wait and show the pictures in person. And, oh, how he was going to enjoy narrating each picture. Danny was like a little kid, grinning and congratulating himself. He would've given anything to have seen the look on Carl's face when he came back looking for his duffle bag. And what must be going through Carl's mind right then.

The next morning, Danny was up and out as easily as a kid on Christmas morning. The snow had stopped, there was no wind and rising sun was igniting some lazy morning clouds when he started home. He did need his snowshoes this trip but they hardly slowed him down and he was home in time for cocktail hour.

"You what?" Cindy asked. They were both in the kitchen, drinks in hand when Danny finally mentioned it.

"I ran into Carl out there."

"Get outta here, really?" Cindy said smiling. "What was he doing out there? Looking for you-know-who or something?"

"No, he wasn't looking, he was... being."

"Huh?"

Danny had milked it long enough, it was show time.

Twenty minutes later, after Cindy had run out of 'I don't believe its', sonofabitches, other swear words and tears, she slumped against Danny; "God, what're we going to do?"

The question stunned Danny. "Whadda we gonna do?"

"Whadda mean, whadda we gonna do? I don't know about you but I'm gonna expose the bastard for the fraud that he is."

Cindy gathered herself for a moment and looked at Danny. "Do you know how embarrassing this will be for the community and for the people who bought into the Bigfoot thing? For the Chamber for-"

"So what? I want---"

"Sure, I can see the headlines now," Cindy said.

"Come see the town of Leavenworth, home of the Sasquatch suckers."

Danny was having a hard time believing what he was hearing. "Please don't tell me you're suggesting I keep these photos to myself?"

Cindy took one of Danny's hands in hers, a sure tell that she was about to ask him to listen for a moment. "Let me play devils' advocate here for a sec, okay?" Danny rolled his eyes but didn't say anything.

"Folks know how you feel about Carl, right? And I know because of the weather and the situation at the time that these photos aren't your best, okay? So then, who's to say you didn't photo shop these, like you accused Carl of doing? The light isn't good in most of the shots, they're blurred and ---

"What? I can't believe that you're gonna defend---

"Stop it! You know I'm not defending Carl, I'm just saying it might be better to think this over a little bit more before we do or say anything."

Danny's disappointment was clear and Cindy did her best to console him. "Listen, honey, Carl has to know that he's been found out, right? Either he noticed the duffle bag was moved or he couldn't find it. Either way he's probably half way to Bolivia right now."

Danny let that soak in. He had planned on

195

going back at some point to see if the bag was still there and if so, bring his trophy home. But now there was a sense of urgency to collect the suit, DNA and all. Cindy leaned him and kissed him. "And then if we do ever hear from him again we can always ask him if he'd like his suit pressed or not."

The next morning was clear and relatively warm as Danny drove to trailhead 103, a trailhead that was much closer to the caverns and caves but a much less scenic route than the one he'd taken on his photo safari. As he pulled into the trailhead, his pulse rate jumped when he saw Carl's van, covered in snow.

Danny parked and as he approached the van he noted that there weren't any footprints around it. He peered inside but couldn't see much. He pounded on the door but got no response. Then he really pounded on the door, hoping to dent it.

With his anger somewhat sated, Danny set off hiking toward the cavern by approaching it from the opposite direction he had three days earlier. An hour after leaving the trailhead he could see the tree where

Carl had done his little dance gyrating as Bigfoot. Danny went into a stalkers mode and as he drew nearer to the tree he could see footprints leading away from it. Keeping the rise and boulders between him and the cavern, Danny circled to his left and gradually climbed up over rocks to where he was looking slightly upward towards the cliffs and ridge. Sunlight had had yet to reach the back walls of the grotto but Danny could make out a figure bent over something in the shadows. Its head resembled the one Carl had for his Bigfoot suit and was gyrating and bobbing around like it was pulling at something with its mouth.

Just then Carl's parka floated into the sunlight and landed on the rocks near Danny. A second later one of his boots thudded on top of it. Danny moved away from his hiding spot, started up the slope and called out. "Hey, Carl! Getting dressed again? Are you decent?"

A guttural howl cascaded out of the cavern and another boot flew out towards Danny. The figure stood up, head gyrating, bellowed again and then quickly made its escape, seemingly disappearing in the

197

rocks and crevices. Then, Danny noticed something sticking out of the boot near him; it was bloody and looked like a bone. A shinbone... A moment passed before Danny looked back up at the cavern, then he called out again, "Yo!...Carl?

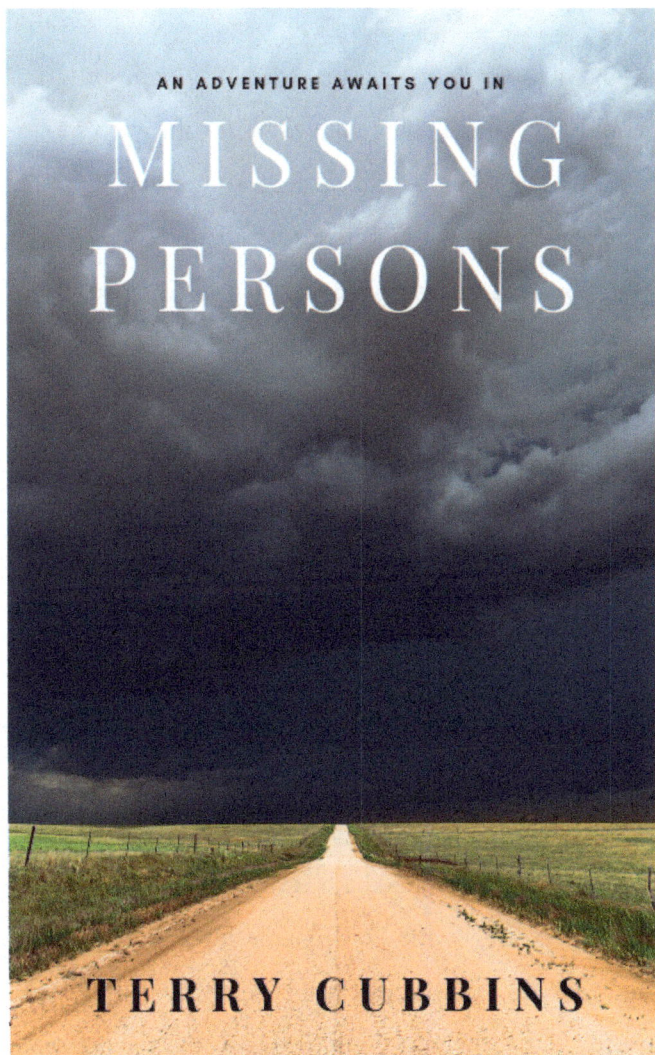

AN ADVENTURE AWAITS YOU IN

MISSING

PERSONS

TERRY CUBBINS

MISSING PERSONS

Silas tried to get his eyes to open, but they wouldn't cooperate. The lids were too heavy. Gravity, too strong. He could smell something though. Something familiar. What was it? His memory pushed hard, but the answer kept dancing away, just out of reach. He floated back to when he was a kid on a lake. He was on a dock. His father was getting a small boat ready. Pulling the starter rope on an outboard motor. Cussing. Blue smoke, with the smell of oil and…gasoline. *Gasoline! That was it!* Silas' eyes popped open but his sense of smell quickly gave way to a blurry visual; a twisted black panel full of gauges and dials. Broken glass. A red knob. He leaned his head back, closed his eyes again and rested for a moment.

When he opened his eyes again, he gradually became aware of the instruments in front of him. A fuel gauge… Cylinder head temp… Altimeter… rpms. All the needles and arrows in the gauges were frozen in place.

Another whiff of gasoline brought him completely awake. He was alone. Strapped in a seat. In an airplane. In a... crashed airplane. He looked down at his legs and feet. He moved them. He wiggled his fingers in his lap. Then, gently he brought his hands to his head. Everything seemed to be in place. Nothing seemed to hurt. Looking through a broken windscreen and past a crumbled propellor, he took in the surrounding terrain. Scattered forest. Mostly level ground. It was daylight, but no sun. More of a burnt overcast. Afternoon, maybe. Then his eyes were drawn to a thin line of black smoke slowly snaking up from the engine cowling.

That's when it all came together for Silas. Well, almost. Hurriedly, he clicked open his seat belt and reached for a door handle on his left. He started to panic when he couldn't immediately find a handle and then he remembered; he was in a single-engine, low-wing Cherokee 140. Entry and egress were done through a door on the passenger's side. He lunged across the passenger's seat, opened the door and stepped out onto a mostly intact wing, then it was a short hop to the ground. He wobbled a few steps away from the plane before looking back. Flames were now driving the smoke up from the engine compartment. Then, just as he was getting used to consciousness, the plane exploded sending him into the base of a large pine tree.

This time, Silas groaned himself awake, knowing his five-foot-ten; forty-three year old, 170-pound body had been in a wreck. His short clipped brown hair, singed even shorter by the explosion. There was a knot on his forehead that wasn't there before. Slowly he sat up and looked around. *Wait. Where am I again?* He rubbed his eyes. *I crashed the goddamn plane, right? Where'n the hell is it then?* From where he sat he could see fifty feet through the evergreen trees in every direction, but no sign of a wreckage. He pulled out his cell phone that was remarkably still in his pocket. No Service.

The last thing he remembered was taking off

from Boeing Field in Seattle and flying southeast toward Mt Rainier. He had recently started taking flying lessons and had soloed with about 12 hours in the cockpit. The Student Pilot license he held meant he could fly by himself but couldn't take anyone with him, other than an instructor. That was okay with Silas, the fewer people around him, the better. He hadn't filed a flight plan because he wasn't really going anywhere in particular, just building up his hours and getting away from the madding crowds. Flying was his way of getting away from people. He recalled flying parallel with Interstate 90 and looking down at the traffic below. Thousands of cars and trucks, antlike, clogging the roads and highways, desperately scrambling towards their destinations as if to stay ahead of a tsunami. Silas just shook his head. Disgusting. Busy, busy, busy. Hurry, hurry, hurry. He remembered he had only been in the air for about fifteen minutes when he became aware of the thunderhead clouds south of Mt Rainer. Inept meteorologist again. Subsequently, he had begun a slow, 180-degree turn… then, blip. That's all he could remember.

Now, he stood up, took a few tentative steps forward and stopped. His right ankle hurt like hell and he couldn't put much pressure on it. He knew he should stay near the wreckage but, *where in the hell was it? Where was he?* He considered his situation. He wanted to explore his surroundings, as for all he knew, he could be close to a road or cabin or something. But it was getting dark fast and with a bum wheel, he knew he wouldn't get far. *Maybe I should think about building a lean-to or something. Some kind of shelter.* As he looked around, he saw that there were plenty of branches and boughs within limping distance. The design engineer side of him took over and soon he had a shelter drawn up in his mind.

Thirty minutes later, he sat down and admired his work. Sticks and stones and boughs and branches, all piled tee-pee style against the base of a large pine tree. As he sat there, a thought occurred to him, *this housing might just be what I need. A damn building inspector will probably show up and wanna see a building permit.* Silas didn't move for a long time, just sat, watching and listening. There was no moon, no stars, no sounds. The encompassing darkness had the look and feel of used steel wool. He thought a fire would be nice, but he didn't have any matches and didn't think he could do the rubbing-sticks-together thing. It was too bad, because like the building inspector notion, Silas assumed if he did get a fire going someone would pop up to tell him campfires were not allowed in the area. He checked his phone again but still, 'No Service.' Finally, with nothing else to do, he crawled into his bunker. He shoved some loose dirt and pine needles around, laid down and scooted his butt and body into position, then closed his eyes. He knew sleep would be sketchy at best and probably not happening anytime soon.

Silas willed his eyes to stay closed but they fluttered open every three seconds. The only sounds he could hear were coming from within his head. As he lay there, he thought of his ex-wife, Patti and what she would think of his situation now. They had met while working at Microsoft. They were design engineers, single, in their twenties and both impulsive as hell. Once their romance started, it wasn't long before they bought a small travel trailer and dashed off to Reno and got married. From Reno, they had driven north, naively thinking they might stop and camp at Yellowstone National Park for a few days. *Yeah, sure. Just park er' anywhere.* They did make it to Yellowstone but at the entry kiosk, a Park Ranger asked them, "Do you have reservations?"

Patti leaned past Silas and smiled up at the man, batted her blues, and asked, "Sir, can we just make reservations now? We're on our honeymoon."

The Ranger tipped his Smoky Hat and said, "I'm sorry, ma'am, we're full up for the year. But you can reserve a site now, you know, for your first-year anniversary?"

When they motored up to Montana's Glacier National Park, it was more of the same. There was no more room to camp in the 1583 square mile park. No

Vacancy. Full up. One night they thought they'd found a place to camp in Idaho, but the next morning the ticket on their windshield said they owed $50 for not displaying the proper permit. Signs, signs, everywhere a sign. Do this, don't do that. Can't you read the signs? By the time they'd returned to Seattle they had spent more nights 'camped' in rest areas than in a forest, sounds of idling truck diesel engines lulling them to sleep.

Their marriage had gotten off to a rocky start and it wasn't long before the two wondered if they hadn't of acted in haste. Their immediate environment didn't help. Seattle traffic was getting worse. Real estate prices and rentals were sky high. Protests in the streets daily. Homeless people bothering people. Homeless people bothering other homeless people. News. Traffic again. And, in Patti's view, Silas had hardened and grown bitter. He wasn't as fun as he used to be. She quit going to Seahawk games with him after he got in a fight with a drunken fan and they were all asked to leave. He gave up golf because the courses had become so crowded that a round of golf took five hours or more. 'Thanks Tiger', he would say. While driving his car, he was constantly looking in the rearview mirror daring someone to tailgate so he could give them a brake. He started calling out people for not putting their shopping carts away. For Silas, it was all about respect and he felt he wasn't getting his fair share. Still, Patti hung in there. They had talked about raising a family before they were married and Silas was agreeable then but now had distanced himself from the idea. Having a child became a touchy subject with them. Once, after a particularly contentious argument, Silas had said, "There's just too many damn people in the world as it is." That was finally enough for Patti. After six years of marriage, she filed for divorce, citing the ever-popular phrase, 'irreconcilable differences.' Now, lying in his shelter, Silas's brain uncontrollably ran the gauntlet of memories both good and bad for hours. Then, just before daylight, fatigue caught up with him and he finally dropped off. He dreamed about the ringing sound a telephone makes when there's a telemarketer waiting on the other end. The dream looped over and over...

When he finally dragged himself out of his shelter, he was looking at the same, dull overcast sky as the day before. Nothing had changed. No sign of a crashed plane. No phone service. Silas took a leak and made a decision; he'd search for the wreckage in the direction he felt it most likely to be, if he couldn't find it there, he'd keep walking until he found something, anything. If rescuers weren't smart enough to locate him, he'd rescue himself. Piss on 'em.

He had only taken a few steps when he noticed something on the ground ahead of him. It was a sheen of color like that of gasoline on water. When he drew closer, the sheen suddenly burst skyward, forming a curtain of red, yellow and green effervescent lights dancing around like an aurora borealis. Silas was stunned initially and quickly backed up a few steps. As he did, he noticed that the lights seemed to diminish. Was this the vestige of the

209

wreckage? When he started forward again, the lights got brighter and he got warmer. A few more steps and Silas's skin began to tingle and he noticed a smell of sulfur in the air. He backed off again and the lights dimmed again. The column of lights, colors and whatever else it was, was only about twenty feet wide but when Silas tried to go to his left, around them, the whole thing shifted as if to block him off. He went to his right and the same happened. The only direction it seemed he could travel was back the way he came.

Silas returned to his shelter and constructed a makeshift crutch out of a tree branch. He took one last look at where'd he just been, drew a breath, and set off in the opposite direction. He made his way through the scattered forest without any other encounters of the weird kind.

Twenty minutes later the terrain opened up and Silas found himself standing on a ridge overlooking a large, crater-like valley.... A crater-like valley with a small town right in the middle of it. Silas almost cried.

"See! There's a freaking town right there for

Christ sake! I knew it!" He was about two miles from the town but he yelled out anyway. "Hey, down there! You guys lookin' for me?... Hey! Look! Up here!" He waved his arms over his head. "Yoo-hoo!" He checked again for phone service. No deal. He stared down at the little burg and noted that there was only one road into it. He didn't see any traffic on the road but that didn't surprise him. The town didn't look big enough to hold more than a few hundred people. It would be nice if one of them was a doctor, but as long as he could make a phone call and get something to eat and drink, he'd be fine for the time being.

After surveying what looked like the best route to take down to the town, Silas set off again, help within sight now. He smiled to himself as he hiked down through sparse forest. He pictured the storyline in his head, *'Pilot survives crash in wilderness. Walks out on his own.'* He wondered if he should ditch the crutch before he saw anyone. *Nah, the story works better with it. But, what about the weird shit? How do I explain that? Nothing's happened since, right? Maybe I had a concussion.*

Maybe I better not say anything about it for now.

An hour later, when Silas emerged from the trees he found himself looking at the back sides of small, one story houses. All look a-likes. Asphalt shingle siding. Old brick chimneys. Fenced backyards. Children's swing sets. A dog kennel for Buddy. *Must be a mining town, coal or something. How come I don't know about this place? Spent all my life in the state, I should have at least a guess as to where I am?* He walked past a few more backyards before it dawned on him that he had yet to see any activity. No children playing, no Buddy barking. He followed the row of houses until he came to a corner where he turned left onto a side street. He was somewhat relieved to see a couple of cars and pickups parked along the curbs on both sides of the street. Two blocks ahead he could see a traffic light at an intersection. It was an unblinking red. As he drew closer, he could see that there was no traffic waiting for the light to change. Kitty-corner across the street was a gas station/minimart with a silver SUV parked at the pump. As crossed the intersection, he looked both ways. To his right there were just a few old wooden structures on both sides of the street that looked like they might house and old car or two. Beyond that a sign that read, *Dead-End*. The street to his left, had a dozen or more old wooden buildings with false storefronts. There were a few cars and pickups parked along the street for about a half a mile where the town looked like it ended. Still no people in sight. Has the town been evacuated? Did St. Helens blow again? An active volcano could explain some things. Silas walked up to the SUV at the pump but there was no one in it. He went up to the front door of the station and pulled it open.

"Hello?" but nobody was home. There wasn't even anything on the shelves. He made his way back to the restrooms marked For Customers Only.

"Hello?" he opened the doors. *Nada. Am I in a movie? Is this a movie set?* He went back outside and looked inside the car at the pump. There was a key in the ignition. Silas got in, tried to start the car but nothing happened. Not even the clicking of a weak battery. As he sat there, he looked across the street and saw a general store. He knew it was a general store because the flaking painted sign above the entry sign read, General Store.

By now he was starting to drag his right foot a little more and it took him a while to get back across the street. He should have saved himself the trouble. The scene was the same. Door unlocked, no goods anywhere, no body to be seen. Outside the store was a battered, lime green, 1950 GMC pickup. There was a key in the ignition. Silas checked it out. No luck, no juice. *Hey, this is a stick shift. Maybe I can roll this enough to pop the clutch, start the fucker.* Problem was, because of his weaken condition and throbbing ankle, he needed an incline of some degree, either forward or back, but the ground all around him was flat as pee on a plate.

He started walking again, toward the end of town. Along the way, he stuck his head into a drug store and a laundromat. His own voice echoed back to him when he called out. Silas walked down the middle of Main Street bewildered with his surroundings and situation. Then, just as he went past the last building in town, he spotted something familiar puddled on the road ahead. A slick of colors like gas on water. *Same weird shit as before.* As he drew nearer the colors morphed upwards and outward, barring his way. *What is this?* Frustrated, Silas studied the obstacle for a moment then, made a decision. *Screw it. I'm going through it this time.* He put his head down and began walking hard toward it. He huffed and puffed, but couldn't seem to get any closer to it. It was like he was walking the wrong way on a moving escalator.

Finally, exhausted, he gave up his effort and backed away. It was beginning to get dark. He needed rest. Dejectedly, he turned around and started walking back toward the town and that's when he noticed the city limit sign...

WELCOME TO
HELL

POPULATION
0

AN ADVENTURE AWAITS YOU IN

DOING TIME

TERRY CUBBINS

DOIN' TIME - *A True Story*

In July of 1986, as I was sitting at the defense table in the San Francisco Federal Court House, my lawyer leaned over and whispered, "Remember now, when Judge Snocke says something to you, you just say, 'yes sir, or no sir.' That's it. Don't give him any reason to add to the sentence we've already agreed upon, okay?"

Made sense to me. Judge Fred Snocke, who was known for his lack of sense of humor, had weeks earlier, sentenced three of my co-defendants to significant jail time. We were all meeting like this because on May 19th of that year, I was aboard a 120' workboat with three other crewmembers returning to San Francisco from Thailand when the U.S. Coast Guard saw fit to board us. We were carrying over seventeen tons of Thai-weed valued at fifty-million dollars. I don't know what the average age is for a first-time felony arrest, but at forty, I'm guessing I was a little older than most, but then I always was kind of a slow learner. You'd thought with five years of high school under my belt, I would have known better.

When I finally did graduate high school, I served in the Navy aboard an aircraft carrier in Viet Nam, followed by a stint in Puerto Rico and Cuba as crew chief in an anti-submarine patrol squadron flying P-2V's. After being discharged from the Navy, I applied for work with Crowley Maritime, a tugboat/towboat outfit in Seattle. I assured Crowley management that I had been an engineer in the Navy, leaving out the part about being a flight engineer.

In 1970, after a year or so working on the tugs, I got a call from my older brother, Tim, saying he'd found a town in the Rocky Mountains that was wide open with lots of spirited women and none were ugly. As it was, the maritime union I belonged to had just gone on strike, so, I left Seattle and joined my brother in Aspen, Colorado.

Tim was right about the women and the town was wide open. I took a job as a carpenter, working on a few spec custom houses that were funded almost causally with dusty money stemming from the marijuana trade. Marijuana movers in town were viewed more like rum runners supporting the local economy. Often, when a house we were working on was finished, we received bonuses in pot. Through osmosis, I eventually picked up enough smuggling skills, that when combined with my maritime experience, helped set my course to the jailhouse.

The Panamco II was the name of the boat in question and of the four crewmen, I was the only one to make bail thanks to my mother putting up her modest home in Seattle as collateral. The captain had been taken to parts unknown to be questioned, while the two deck hands, who were brothers from Canada, cooled their heels in a cell together awaiting sentencing. As the wheels of justice rolled on, the captain made a deal with the prosecutors by giving up some people who had apparently hung him out to dry on a previous pot run. Despite the captain's cooperation, Judge Snocke sentenced him to ten years in prison. However, just before the captain was sentenced, he testified that the crew were initially hired to deliver the boat to a buyer in Singapore and then bring another ship back to the U.S. He told prosecutors that he hadn't divulged to the rest of us that we would be stopping on the way back to pick up a load of pot. It sounded pretty lame, but it was something.

As a crew we were grateful for the captain for his testimony, but we didn't hold out much hope that anyone would believe him. The prosecution grilled us, "If you didn't know about the pot in the beginning, why didn't you munity later, after you learned what was going on? Three against one, right?"

"It's against maritime law," we meekly offered.

When prosecution investigators pointed out that maritime law has provisions regarding illegal activities, and ignorance was no excuse, we ad-libbed, and said, "The captain told us that if we loaded and off-loaded on the high seas, we weren't under U.S. jurisdiction and weren't breaking any laws."

The investigators didn't say anything but their smirks said; "Plu-leese."

After a long silence, one of the sailors added, "Oh, yeah... we didn't how to navigate either."

Surprisingly, the prosecution seemed to brush away our weak narrative and instead, offered us a deal; if we would plead guilty to a charge of 'Illegal Use of a Communication Facility (VHF radio) in Connection with a Smuggling Operation', and waive our 'Right of Discovery,' they would drop the conspiracy charges plus what seemed to be about 97 other indictments against us. I had no clue what Right of Discovery meant. For all I knew, 'Discovery' was the name of a town, and we were just to the right of it. My lawyer explained; "It means that the prosecution is obligated to disclose what led to your arrest. In other words, they gotta tell you how you you caught you."

"Okay, so?"

"So, in some cases the prosecution would rather not disclose that information. For instance, they may have an undercover operative or a snitch in the field who they want to keep employed. So, they offer you a deal."

He paused to let that sink in for a moment, "And the deal is four years in prison followed by five years of probation."

Four years might seem like a long time, especially if measured in todays' political terms, but when we were initially arrested, there was talk of 15 to 20 years for each of us. That meant I could miss all of middle age and not pick up again until I was old.

So? We took the four years, hoping to be out in three and a half for good behavior. The Canadians were sentenced and immediately shipped to Canada while I remained out on bail awaiting sentencing.

Then, a strange thing happened. Two days after the sailors arrived in Canada, they were released by Canadian officials and ordered to begin their five-year probation. When my lawyer heard of what happened with the Canadians, he was like wet on water, arguing that my degree of culpability was the same as theirs and that I should be given the same consideration when I was sentenced.

Maybe it was because the authorities had gotten all they could have out of the captain and saw me as just a dumb shit and probably not a repeat offender, or maybe they were just tired of my lawyer, but in the end, another arrangement was made; I would be sentenced to four years, but in lieu of going 'behind the wall' in a real prison, I would serve six months in a minimum-security federal prison camp and then be released to start five years of probation. It was made clear to me that if I screwed up for any reason while in the camp, I'd spend the next four years behind-the-wall. I was pretty sure I could handle the six months. I was even allowed to request one of the minimum-security prisons within a few hours' drive from where I lived.

At the time, I was living in Solana Beach, California, with my brother and his girlfriend, Julie. My first choice for a federal prison camp was in Lompoc, near Santa Barbara, but at the time they were full- up with white collar criminals and no longer taking reservations. The only other federal minimum-security prison in Southern California then was Boron FPC in the Mojave Desert, so that's what I requested. No ocean view, but what's a guy to do?

When Judge Snocke finally arrived in the courtroom and settled in his seat, the court reporter read the indictment against me, and then it was Snocke's turn. He took his time looking at some statements on his desk before addressing my lawyer.

"So, counselor, you're telling this court that when your client was hired as the engineer on the boat, he and the other two crewmembers were not aware that they would be bringing marijuana back until after they'd refueled and left the dock in Malaysia? You're also telling this court that one of the reasons the crew didn't munity was because they didn't know how to navigate? Says here, sir, your client served in the navy aboard ships and aircraft, worked on ocean going tugboats, took courses in astronomy and has a private pilot's license. None of these endeavors necessarily qualifies him as being smart, the fact that he's here today kind of answers that question, but I'm guessing he could find north if he really had to?"

My lawyer just shrugged and said nothing. My heart rate went up. Did the judge not get the memo about the discovery dealie and the Canadians?

Snocke looked straight at me, "And why in the world would anyone want to go out to the desert in Boron?"

I felt he was asking me a direct question and before my brain could get in touch with my mouth, I blurted, "I'd rather not go anywhere, your Honor." I was just being honest.

My lawyer stiffened and suddenly everything stopped in the courtroom. And then, Snocke did something out of character, he took off his glasses, rubbed his eyes... and chortled. Behind me I heard a few nervous snickers bounce around the courtroom. Then Snocke put his glasses back on, picked up the gavel and ordered me to self-surrender at Boron Federal Prison Camp on November 1, 1986, to begin a six- month sentence.

Boron Federal Prison Complex was formerly a

U.S. Air Force facility near Edwards Airforce Base in the Mojave Desert. Most of the buildings used by the Air Force remained in place including a huge radar dome that sat atop a hill at the north end of the facility. Buildings and barracks at Boron that once housed officers and enlisted men, now held between 500-700 inmates. A cyclone fence enclosed the nearly one hundred acres of what some folks called, 'Club Fed.'

Not to be confused with 'Club Med', Boron was surrounded by sagebrush and desert inhabited by rattlesnakes, scorpions, foxes, coyotes, packrats and lizards. Summer temperatures on the high desert reached 115 degrees in summer and strong winds of fifty-miles per hour could blow cold in winter.

On Nov 1, my brother and I began the drive to my temporary digs in the desert. The last leg of the journey, on Hiway 395, we noticed signs warning passing motorists not to pick up hitchhikers.

Just north of Cramer Junction we turned east off of Hiway 395 onto a cracked asphalt road with a sign; 'Boron Federal Prison. Entrance One mile'. Twenty-feet past that sign, another sign, stacked with tumble weeds against one side of it read, 'Dead End.'

In the distance we could see the white radar dome perched on a knoll above the compound. As we drew closer, we saw seven or eight wooden barracks and two larger brick buildings inside the compound.

The road ended in a cul-de-sac that fronted a wire gate on wheels. An American flag hung limp over a small wooden building next to the gate. A single sign on the door of the building read, 'Boron Federal Prison. No Trespassing.'

After saying goodbye to my brother, I walked through the entry door to start the clock. I stepped up to an unmanned counter and watched two women at individual desks typing away. Finally, one of them looked up and asked, "May I help you, sir?"

Channeling Cool Hand Luke, I asked, "Is this the University of Boron?"

"No sir, this is a Federal Prison Camp," the woman said, somewhat proudly, then went back to her typing.

The woman let me sweat like a stand-up comedian

who had just bombed, before she looked up again. I meekly waved my surrender papers. That was enough to bring her up to the main desk. She took my papers and gave them a look.

"Is there any reason why you shouldn't be here?"

"Huh?"

"Do you know anyone in this camp?

"What? No, I don't know anybody here." Is this where they apologize and send me home? I thought of my Canadian friends.

"Have you testified against anyone who might be incarcerated here?"

"No, I've never testified against anyone. Why---"

"Just standard questions. Take a seat, a correctional officer will be right with you.

Within minutes a guard showed up, escorted me to a small, delousing room where he ordered me to strip. After looking in every orifice on my body with a flashlight, I was issued the standard prison garb; a winter coat, two pairs of pants, two short sleeved shirts, two long sleeved, all in a stylish olive drab and complimented by black lace-up brogans. Among our personal items we were allowed to bring; toothbrush, disposable razor, underwear and a lightweight robe.

After my fitting, the guard said, "Okay, let's go see the Captain." For a moment I thought he meant the captain of the Panamco 11, but I soon learned different. The guard, or 'hack,' as they were called by prisoners, led me to a brick admin building where the Captain, aka, the Warden, gave myself and three other newbies the lowdown on what he expected from us.

"This is a labor camp and everyone is expected to work while they're here. We'll try to assign you something that fits your work history, if you have any, or you can choose to rake rocks every day, or rake and bake as they call it here, it's up to you. One way or another, you will work eight hours a day. You will also be counted at least six times a day to make sure you're still breathing.

"I will also tell you that you can probably find a way to escape this camp if you look hard enough. We don't run a chain-gang or have any bloodhounds and we won't chase after you if you run. There's no drinking water for miles and just too many dang old snakes and scorpions out there for us to want to go look for you. And remember, if you do run, eventually you'll get caught and you'll never see minimum security again."

My next stop was the barracks where I'd be housed along with about ninety other inmates. On the walk over, I noticed several inmates raking dirt and small rocks around the barracks. It had to be about 95 degrees outside and they didn't appear to be happy in their work.

Rooms in the barracks were 12x12ft spaces with two bunkbeds, a small desk and two straight back wooden chairs. Next to each bunk there was a coat rack and a small storage locker. The guard looked at his watch and said, "Tomorrow morning, after chow, be outside at the front steps for your job assignment for the day. Most likely you'll be raking and bakin' til we check you out further. Stay here for now, your roommates are getting off work and will be here in about five minutes. You got any questions about how things work around here, just ask Dutch."

"Dutch?"

"Yeah, Dutch Schultz. Past President of the Hells Angels, San Diego Chapter. One of your roommates. His first name is really Eugene, but I wouldn't call him that if I were you."

The guard left and I sat down on one of the bunks. Five minutes later my new roomies walked in the room. A tall, lanky guy who looked to be in his thirties walked in first and introduced himself, "I'm Tom but you can call me Cowboy." Then turning to a shorter man behind him; "And this guy here is Earl. He don't say much, but when he does, you can believe it." To prove his point, Earl, who looked a little like Robert Di Niro, just nodded and said nothing. The last man in the room came up behind Cowboy and pushed him out of the way. Big man, 6'1" muscular build, 35-ish, had long brown hair and a beard. Looked like he could be a rassler on TV. "I'm Dutch. That's my bunk you're sittin' on."

Righto. I quickly moved out of his way. He glared at me, "What's your beef, man?"

"Huh? I, uh, I got no beef..." Jeesh, is this where

232

the shank comes out?

Cowboy laughed and jumped up on the bunk above Mr. Schultz and said to me, "He wants to know what'd you-all get busted for?"

"Oh, yeah, pot. A pot bust," I said, starting to feel a little better about the situation. All criminals and Harley riders smoke pot, right? Wait till I tell them how much pot I got caught with. Maybe they'll offer me a lower bunk.

"How much pot they bust you with?" Dutch asked.

"Little over seventeen tons," I said. I stood a little taller and casually shrugged.

"So, how long you down for?"

"Umm, down for?"

"Yeah, how much time you get?"

As soon as I said, 'six months,' all conversation stopped. Earl looked at Dutch. Cowboy stuck his head over his bunk and looked down at Dutch. Dutch stared at me. When the conversation did pick up again, I wasn't included in it.

My first night in Boron F.P. Camp was mostly a sleepless one, but at least it was out of the way and in the morning, I mentally clicked one day off the calendar. As I stood in the chow line for breakfast, I noticed other inmates were chatting with each other, but when I tried to say something to the guy behind me about the weather, he grunted and looked away.

After the morning meal, which was surprisingly good, I reported for my first day of work as ordered. I was given a steel rake and assigned a patch of dirt and tiny gravel on the sunny side of the barracks. If I thought I'd have a chance to talk to some fellow workers I was mistaken. I was the Lone Raker.

However, when I looked over to the next barracks, I saw a rather dignified-looking, silver-haired inmate standing there, holding a rake. I took a chance and waved. He immediately gave me the finger, tossed his rake to the ground and sat down on a bench. It wasn't long before a hack showed up and led the man away. Later, I heard that the distinguished looking man was mob connected and apparently felt that manual labor was below his strata.

In the short time that I had been in Boron I had learned that some of the prisoners there had already done hard time in other prisons for crimes like wire fraud, embezzling, bank robbery and other federal crimes. Some had been transferred from medium security to Boron to begin acclimating for their release back into society, almost like a half-way house. As far as the mob guy was concerned, apparently status was more important than sense.

My status of being shunned continued for three days, however, on the fourth day, my fortune changed. While standing in line for lunch outside the chow hall, I thought I recognized someone ahead of me. When he turned around to say something to the guy behind him, I could see it was Billy Sullivan, a happy-go lucky guy I knew from Aspen. Sully, as every one called him, had been a waiter in a popular restaurant in town and some of the deserts that he touted came with the option of a gram of cocaine if you had an extra Franklin in your pocket. When he saw me, he yelled, "Hey! What the hell...?" He quickly gave up his place in line and joined me.

The chow hall was set up like a cafeteria, and after we took our trays through the chow line, we grabbed a table with two empty seats and caught up on things. He was doing a year and a day for selling coke and then I told him my story. He was duly impressed with the weight and even more impressed with my light sentence. Then he proceeded to give the low-down on the camp. "For one thing, you won't find any rocket scientists in here." he said. An inmate who was sitting at the same table looked puzzled, then proved Sully's point by asking, "Why would there be any rocket scientists in here?" The nearest thing to a celebrity incarcerated at Boron at that time was Wayne Newton's brother. Maybe this was him.

When I told Sully which barracks and room I was in, he said, "You're in with Dutch Schultz? You've either got the best seat in the house or the worse." Then I mentioned the conversation I had with Dutch when I first met him and how it ended. Sully laughed.

"Well, no shit, pal. Dutch probably assumes you ratted out someone to get the sentence you got. Dutch is not a bad guy once you get to know him but the one thing he hates most in life is a rat or a snitch."

Well, duh.

"But, don't worry, Dutch has a way of finding out about somebody through his lawyer in San Diego. He's probably getting you checked out as we speak. If you're still alive and in the same room with Dutch by the end of the week, everyone will know you're okay."

When I returned to my barracks that day after work, it was clear the atmosphere had changed. Dutch smiled and wanted to hear all about my voyage on the Panamco 11. Ten minutes later, we were like old friends. I even had the courage to ask, "What's your beef, man? How long you down for?" I stopped short of calling him Eugene, though.

He explained how a snitch ratted him out for bringing Mexican weed across the border. He even told me about his legitimate work he had been doing that involved the Hell's Angel's providing security at music concerts. At that point in our conversation, Dutch got up, went to his locker and pulled out an envelope. Then he sat back down on his bunk and patted a spot next to him. "Here, let me show you some pictures."

Righto. I dutifully sat down on Dutch Schultz's bunk with him. But that wasn't the only surprise coming. When he showed me a picture of him and a friend standing with Tanya Tucker, I thought I recognized his friend. "He looks just like a guy I was in the navy with," I said. "We worked the flight deck together on the USS Enterprise in '65. He played guitar and on our off time he taught me some cords. What's your friend's name?"

"Rod Harris," Dutch said.

"Harris? Oh, I guess that's not…" Then, boom, it hit me: The guy I knew was named Rodney Zabish. I used to kid him about his name, telling him he'd have to either become a comedian or change his name if he wanted to be famous. I asked Dutch, "Does your friend here, have a tattoo of a heart with guitar strings running through it on his right shoulder by any chance?"

Dutch looked at me for a second. Then he pulled another picture out and handed it to me. It was a photo of Dutch and 'Rod Harris' wearing tank tops as they were setting up musical equipment on a stage. You could clearly make out the tattoo of a big red heart with guitar strings on Harris's right shoulder.

On Monday, after a weekend of lounging around the barracks watching football and chatting with my fellow inmates, I began my new job as tool manager in a small, wire cage located on the ground floor of the radar dome on the hill. At eight o'clock in the morning, inmates would line up outside my gage to check out tools for the day. Now, the only time I touched a rake was when I handed it to someone else.

The tools that I was in charge of were of the garden variety type. Besides rakes, there were shovels, hammers, pipe wrenches, pliers, screw drivers and chisels. Everything a guy could want to make a hole in a fence. I even had hacksaw frames, but no blades. That's where the authorities drew the line. If someone wanted an actual blade for a hacksaw, they had to get it from the hack on duty.

The paved road leading up the hill from camp looped around the dome and returned down to the main camp and measured almost a mile. It was a pretty good chug going up the hill, while going down the other side there were workout stations, parallel bars, chin-up bars, places to do push-ups. At the bottom of the road there was a semi-enclosed area with weights, a couple of tread mills along with a heavy bag and a speed bag. One evening I noticed Sully working out there so I joined him. Three nights later, my back went out.

As I hobbled back to the barracks that night, Sully told me about an inmate called Doc. He had been a chiropractor on the outside and was two barracks down from me. He described the guy and suggested I ask him for help. I found the guy alright but when I asked him if his name was Doc, he took one look at me and told me to get the hell away from him. Back in my room, Dutch asked me what I did to my back, "Lifted something wrong, I guess. Maybe a hot shower will help." I grabbed my robe and left the room. When I came back, Doc was in the room with Dutch. "You should've told me you had insurance," Doc said. Before I could answer, he instructed me to lie down on the floor and said, "Prison rules says I can't touch anybody in here, so, let's get this done before a hack comes by."

Doc pushed and poked and twisted me around like all good chiropractors do and when he finished, said, "Drink lots of water and walk some laps on the hill when you can."

After Doc left, Dutch smiled and said, "It's good to have friends in low places."

I took Doc's advice and began walking the hill in earnest in the evenings and weekends. Sully was usually on the hill doing the same thing so we'd walk together, talk about our days in Aspen and catch up on the latest camp gossip. One evening while we were taking laps, he surprised by asking, "You into martial arts now or something?"

"Whaddya talkin' about?"

"Rumor has it that you've got a black robe with Chinese writing on the back of it, like you might be a black belt or something."

I laughed and then explained. "I have a black robe that I brought with me because it's light and easy to pack. I bought it as a souvenir when I was in Hong Kong years ago, but I never wear it. Not sure what caricatures on the back are for, probably good luck or something."

Sully laughed. "Well, your secret is safe with me. News on the prison grapevine travels fast and can elevate your status in camp, or lessen it. Unless someone asks you about it, I'd just go with the flow and leave it alone."

Sully was quiet for a while then said, "And, I think you just gave me an idea."

"About what?" I asked

"Well, there's a guy in my barracks that's a real

jerk, name's Chuck Fagan, got busted for posing as a cop. Fagan would find out through snitches where and when drug deals were going down, then he'd go in, flash his badge and take the stash and money. If there were women involved, he would promise to keep them outa jail in exchange for sexual favors. He even brags about it, thinks he's a stud. And now everyday he gets to leave here on the bus to Edwards for work detail. Says he's already met a couple of women on the base."

"So, what's your idea?"

Sully looked at his watch, "It's almost count time. I'll tell you tomorrow."

I didn't see Sully until chow the next evening. I saw him sitting with two other guys so I brought my tray over and sat down with them. They were talking football until one of the guys shifted the conversation and tapped into the grapevine. "Hey, you know that guy with the big pompadour in barracks two? Fagan, I think his name is? Anyway, I heard he literally got caught with his pants down in a storage area with another guy out at the base yesterday. No shit."

Sully coughed and almost choked on his food. Twenty minutes later, we were on the hill and he was thrilled. "God, I had no idea the news would travel so fast. I just started that story this morning in chow line."

Just before Thanksgiving I was called to the Chapel on the Hill. It was a small structure that stood alone on outcropping of rock just below the radar dome. It faced to the east as if to welcome the sunrise over the desert each morning. The Reverend in charge was about thirty-five years old, tall, thin and wore a scraggy beard above his white collar. He was seldom seen outside his ministry without a cigarette in his mouth. He looked more like someone who needed saving then the one doing the saving. But when he gave me the news that my grandmother had died, I could feel his compassion. He encouraged me to describe my relationship with her and when I told him she helped raise me, he told me that that qualified me for a forty-eight-hour emergency furlough. Did I want to go? Sure, I said.

The next day, Tim picked me up, we drove to the Burbank airport, and together we flew to Sea-Tac Airport in Seattle. After deplaning, Tim asked if I wanted to duck into a bar for a beer before leaving the airport. Living on the edge, I said yes. That's when I saw a guy who I casually knew from high school and had played a couple of rounds of gold with.

"Hey man. When'd you get out?" he asked.

"Get out?"

"Haven't seen you in a while, figured you'd been in jail."

"Oh, right, well I got out a couple of hours ago." *Heh heh.*

He laughed and said, "Good, maybe we can tee'um up again."

"Yeah maybe."

Neither of us said anything for a moment or two, and then he said, "Actually there's a tournament on Monday to support this years high school reunion. Wanna play?"

"Sorry I can't."

"Why? Parol officer won't let you?"

"Something like that haha."

"You always had a good sense of humor Cubbins. Really, where have you been?"

Without thinking I said, "Boron California."

"Boron? Isn't that down where they used to farm borax, like in the old Twenty-Mule Team television series with Ronald Regan?"

"You're close."

"What do you do there?"

"I manage a small tool outfit."

Fortunately before I dug myself in deeper he nodded, drained the last of his beer and said, "Well I've got a plane to catch. Good to see you again, try and stay outta jail now okay?"

"I will." *For another forty-some hours anyway.*

After my grandmother's funeral, friends and relatives gathered at my mother's house for drinks and reminiscing. I helped by serving as bartender and was able to deflect most questions about my recent whereabouts. I also drank along with others and remembered the advise Sully gave me; "Don't do any drugs while you're out because they'll piss test you when you check back in. You can probably drink a beer or two if you stop drinking about twelve hours before coming back, just remember to flush with lots of water."

I did as advised and cut myself off well in advance of the twelve hour warning and the next morning I began flushing with water, lots of water.

By the time our flight took off I had consumed about ten gallons of water... and that's when my ordeal began. Tim and I had been given different seat assignments and we sat several rows apart. This time I found myself in the window seat next to an elderly Asian woman who didn't speak any English and a man with a brace on his leg occupied the aisle seat. As soon as the plane lifted off I had to pee. Fifteen minutes later, I had to pee again. I asked the man if he wanted to exchange seats but he said no because of his leg and the Asian woman shook her head as if I was asking her for money. After playing musical chairs for two torturous hours, we finally arrived at the Burbank airport where I made a dash for the men's room.

For the drive back to Boron I still had a window seat but at least it was easier to get Tim to stop the car so I could pee alongside the road.

When I finally checked in at boron a guard handed me a bottle to pee in. You'd think I could have pee'd right? Well, an hour and a half later, with the guard still watching, I was finally able to go. Maybe it would be easier if I just stayed in jail.

As time passed, I never really got the feeling that I was doing time, more like spending time. Lots of fresh air, exercise, free rent, good grub and a chiropractor who makes house calls. I was pulling down a prison scale of eighty-eight cents a day and Sully passed along a good book every week, starting with Lonesome Dove, by Larry McMurtry.

Another perk for being at Club Fed was its proximity to Edwards AFB and Rodgers Dry Lakebed where so much aviation history has been made. On any given day you might see and hear the roar of military aircraft prototypes like the B-1 Bomber and other Stealth flying machines buzzing around.

On December 14, 1986, the experimental aircraft, Voyager, took off from Edwards in an attempt to fly around the world without stopping or refueling. Crammed in aboard the ultra light craft were pilots, Dick Rutan and Jeana Yeager. (Jeana had a great last name for the flight but was no relation to Chuck Yeager who broke the sound barrier over Edwards AFB in 1947.)

I wasn't able to see the Voyager takeoff, but nine days later, at 8:00am on December 23rd, I was perched near the radar dome when I saw the Voyager appear in the eastern sky. It was being escorted by three or four chase planes, all with their flaps and landing gear down in order to match the slow pace of the history making aircraft. I watched, mesmerized as the Voyager slowly and elegantly made three low passes above Edwards airstrip before finally touching down safely. It was a moment I'll never forget.

Often a fellow prisoner named Frank would join me and Sully on the hill for a few laps. Frank was about my age, salt and pepper hair and a matching well-groomed beard. He was in good physical shape, had a calm demeanor and never complained about anything. If you had to guess his occupation, doctor or attorney would come to mind. However, Frank was in prison for stealing, or 'boosting' as he called it, slot machines in Las Vegas. He had devised a method of drilling the machines so that the odds were in his favor.

When Frank was initially arrested and locked in a cell, he would get up each morning and play eighteen holes of imaginary golf on different courses he knew. He would start off by swinging an imaginary driver, sense how far he hit it and then pace off the yardage.

Then he'd pull a different club for his next shot and repeat the procedure until he reached the green. On the green he carefully read each putt before pulling the trigger on his imaginary putter. Frank said he went through a pre-shot routine before each swing and usually played the morning round in three hours. He would then have lunch and rest up before playing a different course in the afternoon. Guards and other prisoners thought he was crazy.

When Frank first came to Boron, he was content to rake and bake because he could use the rake to practice his golf swing. The day he sent a rock through his barracks window was the day he got assigned to paint detail where he could work more on his putting stroke.

Frank had been down for two years and had six months to go. I said to him once, "Wouldn't it be nice if you could just push a button and fast-forward to your release date?" He laughed and said, "Hell no, life is too short as it is. As long as I'm able to think and imagine, I want to experience every second of every day. Time is all we have you know? Once she's gone, she's gone, baby." Frank was either a glutton for punishment, or not as crazy as some thought.

Other guys passed the time by talking about their wife's, girlfriends and what they were going to do when they got out. A couple of guys had talked about going to Costa Rica to start up a fishing guide service. They asked if I'd be interested in going in on it. Costa Rica was a place that Tim and I had always wanted to go to, so it was a fun thing to toss around but I was pretty sure nothing would come of it.

I didn't have a wife or girlfriend to think about then, but I had did have to think about what I was going to do when I got out. Tim had borrowed fifty thousand dollars for my legal costs and I had to figure out how to begin to pay that off. I didn't have a job waiting for me or any money in the bank, but I did try to be optimistic; I did the math and figured by the time my six months was up in late April, the federal prison system would owe me over a hundred bucks in back wages! And, from now on, if I ever find myself in a situation, I'll have the wisdom to ask, "What would Frank do?"

On February 2nd, Groundhog Day, I heard my name called over the loudspeaker to report to the administration office. Walking over to the building I had lots of thoughts running through my head. Maybe they were going to give me my three-month pin for completing half of my sentence or something? At least I wasn't being called to the Chaplin's office.

Once inside the office I was greeted by an officious looking gentleman in civilian clothes sitting behind a desk. "Please sit," he said, and indicated a chair in front of his desk. He held a folder in his hand then plopped it down in front of him. "I've been looking at your file and noticed your release date. There's been a mistake."

Aw, shit, here we go.

"Your discharge date falls on Saturday, the 28th,

and it's against prison policy to release prisoners on a weekend. So, we'll move your date up a day to that Friday."

Whew, is that all that this is about?

He picked up a small desk calendar and showed me what he was talking about. "There. See? Friday, the 27th."

I saw that Friday was the 27th alright, but it was the 27th of February. I was confused. I understood leap years but not leap months. What happened to March and April?

He seemed to sense my bewilderment. "We applied the days you were incarcerated after your original arrest and deducted time off for good behavior since you've been here. We've pro-rating your good behavior, so, you need to stay clean for another three weeks, okay?"

There was something about a horse's mouth in play here

"Hmm, well... okay." I figured that Frank wouldn't consider this skipping time or a fast-forward.

I kinda felt guilty telling Dutch and Sully about my new release date but when I did, they laughed and congratulated me. I thanked them for their company and help and thought of another person I should thank before I left. It was the lady in charge of the food at Boron. Her name was Helen and she was a friendly black lady who always appeared calm and in control while patrolling her domain. Her holiday meals were exceptional considering the circumstances and the quality and quantity of the daily grub was appreciated by most of the inmates. In the relatively short time that I had been in Boron, I never saw a fight or even a serious argument and the thought crossed my mind that maybe serving good meals to bad boys had something to do with it.

The morning I was leaving, I bumped into Helen outside the chow hall. I told her I was being released that afternoon and mentioned how much I appreciated her work and the food she served. "Thank you," she said, smiling. Then she peered at me over her glasses, looked me in the eye and said,

255

"But I don't think it's worth coming back for, do you?"

After serving my debt to society by spending a little less than four months in Boron FPC, I walked out of Club Fed and climbed into Tim's car. As we were leaving, I looked back and saw three, white, bare butts pressed against the cyclone fence near the gate. I waved as the butts morphed into Dutch, Sully and Frank.

After a nice weekend at home, I set out Monday morning to get a new passport and copies of my seaman's papers back in order. I knew that Scripps oceanic Institute near San Diego was hiring chief engineers and assistants for their research vessels that were sailing to Tahiti to study underwater volcanoes. I was hoping to get my papers back so I could apply with Scrippts. My Merchant Mariner's card that I carried was 'lost' when the captain of the Panamco 11 ordered the crew to toss all I.D.'s overboard just before the Coast Guard boarded us.

The passport application went fine mainly because there was no box marked, 'Have you ever been arrested for a felony?' But it was a different story at the U.S. Coast Guard station in Long Beach. When I applied for new papers, I answered truthfully, realizing I would have to check that felony box for the rest of my life.

After filling out the paperwork, I was told to wait outside an office while an officer reviewed my application. Within minutes, an Ensign named Cramer (who looked to be about sixteen) called me into his office and began grilling me about the felony. When I told him it was a marijuana bust aboard a ship, he immediately declared that my application for new papers was denied. I half expected that that would be the case but when I got up to leave, I got a real surprise. Ensign 'kid' Cramer told me to sit down, I wasn't going anywhere. When I asked him what he was talking about, he said with great authority, "You're under arrest."

"Under what!?"

"Arrest. You're under arrest."

"What for?"

"Attempted to smuggle marijuana into the United States."

I had been patience up until then, but was starting to lose it. "I've already been arrested for that!'

"Not by me you haven't," he said and stood up to face me.

About that time an officer with Commander bars on his shoulders walked into the room. "There a problem here?"

Before kid Cramer could say anything, I quickly explained why I was there, the job I was hoping to apply for and where I had been for the last four months. The commander studied my application and after a minute said, "Okay. We'll set up a hearing and review board regarding your papers. You'll need to attend the hearing. We'll send the date and information to your current address."

"So, I'm not under arrest?"

"What for?"

Weeks later, when I appeared for the hearing,

the judge denied my application and suspended my papers, saying I would have to wait five years to reapply. The next day I saw an article in the L.A. Times, Coast Guard considering cancelling the annual Christmas boat parade in Newport Beach harbor in order to inspect all the vessels for safety violations. This was the brainchild of non other than Ensign Cramer, aka, Ensign Kid Dumbfuck.

I found work with a local homebuilder and was a year into my probation when the cancer that Tim fought eight years previously returned and claimed his life. He was forty-four. I scattered his ashes in the waters near Seattle. Half expecting Ensign Cramer to show up and issue me with a violation of some sort.

After Tim died, I felt broken to the core. I was rudderless and struggled to make sense of anything. Tim's girlfriend Julie, was a big support for me during these times. One day she said, "I think you should get away. Take a vacation. You got your passport back right?" Julie was also a travel agent and I knew she would get a good price for a ticket if I was able to travel. I would need permission from my probation officer, but felt good about my chances as he had already approved my travel out of state to bury Tim. He also knew that I was a self-surrender to begin with and had returned after being furloughed for my grandmother's funeral and had been released early for good behaviour while in Boron.

A week later, I met with my P.O. and asked him if he thought I could leave the country for a short vacation.

"Where to?" he asked.

"Costa Rica," I answered.

He thought about it for a moment and said, "Let me make a call." Two minutes later, I got the okay. Before I left his office, he handed me an official looking document. "Here. Make sure you have a customs agent sign this when you come back into the States."

About a month later, I flew to Costa Rica, rented a jeep, and drove around the sparsely populated and lush country for ten days. As I traveled, I thought about the tales of early explorers and how they would describe native people as either friendly or hostile. The Costa Rican people, or 'Ticos', as they were called, were definitely friendly. So much so that their small nation didn't see the need for an army.

On the way home, we landed in Houston to clear customs, something that I was dreading. The line for customs was long and I was tired and sweating by the time I made it to an agent. I handed him my passport and set my luggage down next to him. As he started to pop the latches on my suitcase, I remembered the note from my P.O. and quickly handed it to the agent.

"What's this?" he asked.

"It's from my probation officer. He would like you to read and sign it."

The agent looked a little puzzled as he read the document. Finally, he looked up and said, "You're a smuggler?"

"Was," I answered.

The agent quickly signed the letter and snapped

my suitcase shut without looking inside it. He waved me through and said, "Have a nice day."

As I was walking away, it occurred to me that having a note from your P.O. might be a good way to smuggle stuff...

Hmm. I wonder what would Frank do?

Terry Cubbins

After serving in the Navy in Viet Nam, Terry was employed as a tugboat engineer in the Pacific Northwest and later in the oilfields of Alaska.

Following that, he moved inland and worked in the home construction business in Aspen, Colorado during the 70's and later in Southern California in the 80's and 90's.

In 2000, Terry returned to his home state of Washington and built a house in the Central Cascade Mountain range and began another career as a copy writer at a radio station in Ellensburg, WA. Terry shares his home with his lab mix, Scooter. They live close to a blue-ribbon trout stream and an alpine golf course.

To learn more about Terry and his other published works, visit TerryCubbins.com or check out his Facebook page @AuthorTerry

BOOKS BY THIS AUTHOR

SMUGGLERS' BLUES: A MOMOIR

There has been silence for a long time, but now it is time to tell the story...

A true story of a smugglers' adventure covertly transporting seventeen tons of illegal marijuana across the open seas. Bear witness to the highs and lows of our smuggler's dangerous journey as he sets sail from North America to Asia, and back again. Re-live the gritty details of dodging pirates, surviving at sea and the dodgy dealings of silent partners and orders given at the end of a telephone. Celebrate the wild wins and the enjoyment of finding sanctuary in paradise, and hang your head when it all comes to an end.

It's been twenty years since that morning on the deck of the Panamco II when I heard, "Terry Cubbins, you have the right to remain silent...anything you say, can, and will, be held against you..."

THE STRINGER

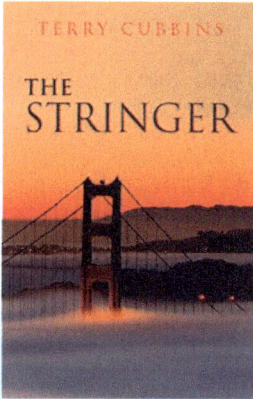

Newly hired at the San Francisco Chronicle, stringer Michael Fletcher is looking to secure the future of his wife and daughter by landing the next big story. But Michael's marriage is tested when sparks fly with Dr. Laurie Scott, who he meets while investigating three professional athletes who died in separate "accidents" over a six-month period. The pressure mounts with the arrival of an encrypted message about the deaths of the athletes that is eerily reminiscent of the work of the Zodiac Killer, who terrorized the Bay Area in the late 1960s. Alone in his pursuit of the source of the cryptic message, Michael must track a potential killer while keeping his marriage intact as his path continues to intersect with that of the beautiful Doctor. Fast-paced crime dramas won't skip a page while solving the mystery of The Stringer.

THERE'LL COME A TIME

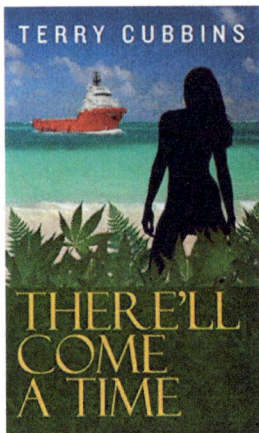

With the war in Viet Nam winding down, navy veteran Sonny Williams returns home to Seattle and learns his older brother, Tim, has been suckered into hauling marijuana for a smuggler known only as 'the old man.' To make matters worse, Tim's kidneys are failing and he will soon need an operation to save his life. To extract his brother from the old man's grip and to raise some fast cash, Sonny makes a one-time deal to sail as the engineer on the Intrepid, a ship that's sailing from San Francisco to Thailand and bringing millions of dollar's worth of pot into the U.S. While the crew of the Intrepid makes repairs and refuels at a small town in Malaysia, Sonny falls in love with a beautiful local woman and vows to return for her once he completes his mission. Murder and betrayal become the game changers that compel Sonny to return to Malaysia on a different ship, not for love, but for vengeance.

LIFE IN THE LEFT-HAND LANE

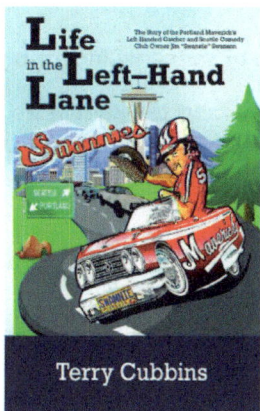

Jim Swanson was a catcher in Little League when a friend told him he should give up the position.

"Why?" Jim asked. His pal clued him, "Because you're left-handed, is why." In high school, Jim's girlfriend observed, "You'll never make varsity as a catcher, you know." Jim asked why not; "Duh! You're left-handed! Hel-loow?"

It wasn't until 1975, after Swanson graduated college with an All-Conference baseball career that someone said, "Hey! You're a left-handed catcher! I can use you!"

The voice belonged to Bing Russell, actor and owner of the Portland Mavericks, an Independent, Single-A team in the Northwest League consisting mostly of misfits who partied hard, ignored traditions, and played loudly. They also beat the Major League franchise teams and set attendance records everywhere they went. Swanson fit right in the team that included

Bing's son, Kurt Russell, and former New York Yankee, Jim Bouton.

Then in 1977, after five years of shenanigans from an independent team with an owner better known as the deputy sheriff on Bonanza, Major League Baseball muscled the Mavericks out of existence.

With the Mavericks gone, Swanson set sail for Seattle, where he kept the party rolling by opening the first underground comedy club in the Northwest called, *Swannies*. A young left-hander named Jerry Seinfeld was Swannies' first act. Ellen DeGeneres and Cheech and Chong soon followed.

Located close to the Kingdome Sports Arena, Swannies became a favorite watering hole for athletes and celebrities. Baseball and comedy. What's not to love?

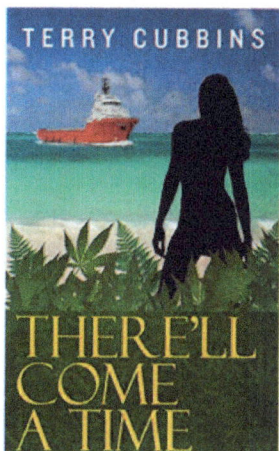

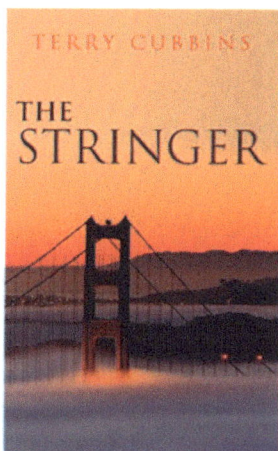

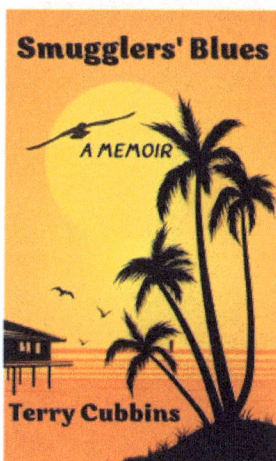

Other works by Terry Cubbins
Find them on Amazon

Made in the USA
Columbia, SC
21 June 2022